The Ghost Horse
of Meadow Green

Anne Louise MacDonald

KCP Fiction

· KCP Fiction is an imprint of Kids Can Press

This is a work of fiction and any resemblance of characters to persons living or dead
is purely coincidental.

Many of the designations used by manufacturers and sellers to distinguish their
products are claimed as trademarks. Where those designations appear in this book
and Kids Can Press Ltd. was aware of a trademark claim, the designations have been
printed in initial capital letters (e.g., Hanoverian).

Kids Can Press acknowledges the financial support of the Government of Ontario,
through the Ontario Media Development Corporation's Ontario Book Initiative; the
Ontario Arts Council; the Canada Council for the Arts; and the Government of
Canada, through the BPIDP, for our publishing activity.

Published in Canada by
Kids Can Press Ltd.
29 Birch Avenue
Toronto, ON M4V 1E2

Published in the U.S. by
Kids Can Press Ltd.
2250 Military Road
Tonawanda, NY 14150

www.kidscanpress.com

Edited by Charis Wahl
Designed by Julia Naimska

Printed and bound in Canada

The hardcover edition of this book is smyth sewn casebound.
The paperback edition of this book is limp sewn with a drawn-on cover.

CM 05 0 9 8 7 6 5 4 3 2 1
CM PA 05 0 9 8 7 6 5 4 3 2 1

National Library of Canada Cataloguing in Publication Data

MacDonald, Anne Louise, 1955–
     The ghost horse of Meadow Green / written by Anne Louise MacDonald.

ISBN 1-55337-636-6 (bound).   ISBN 1-55337-637-4 (pbk.)

I. Title.

PS8575.D618G46 2005   jC813'.54   C2004-902970-3

Kids Can Press is a *Corus*™ Entertainment company

for Frank, for everything

and thanks to Kim for the beginning
and Lana for the end

CHAPTER 1

The Black Horse

Kim leaned her forehead against the school bus window and stared at the horse that ran effortlessly alongside. Today she made him black. She almost always made him black. And she was on that horse, her long golden hair streaming behind her. She rode bareback — no need for saddle or bridle. With touches as light as thoughts, she signaled to him. They sailed over fences, flew with ease through spring green pastures, bounded across driveways without missing a beat. It seemed as if the horse's hooves never touched the ground — like in her dreams. Only today, they ran for the pure joy of it, running toward, not from.

Because today Gramma-Lou was coming. The most wonderful person in the whole world. The only person who loved Kim just as she was. Who never wanted her to be braver or stronger or smarter or taller. Who never ever said she was too shy. "You're very sensitive," Gramma-Lou would say, "and that's not a weakness — that's a strength."

It had been more than a year since Kim had even heard that sweet voice. Gramma-Lou was too sick to talk whenever Kim phoned. That's what Kim's mother had said. Kim knew it was really because her father hated long-distance bills.

But today Gramma-Lou was coming to live in Meadow Green — Kim's dream come true. Kim leaned forward and pushed the black horse to an impossible speed, leaving behind the knowledge that dreams can turn without warning.

She waved to the bus as they galloped along. Admiring faces smiled back at her.

Three girls screamed and jumped to their feet. "Aaagh! A frog!"

Reality landed with a wet *thawk* on the cracked turquoise vinyl seat. Kim jerked her mind back aboard the bus and blinked at the fat green frog crouched by her thigh. It stretched a webbed hind foot forward and squeegeed lint out of one of its glittering yellow eyes.

"Poor thing," she breathed. She reached for the frog to tuck it into the safety of her knapsack.

"Cracker Kid picked it up!"

"Gross. You'll get warts!"

"Hey, Cheese and Crackers, throw it to me!"

"It's a prince. Kiss it! Kiss it!"

Every eye on the bus focused on the frog ... and Kim.

She couldn't breathe. Her heart hammered in her ears. She dropped the frog and spun back to the window. If only she could throw herself through it. Jump out and find a hole to crawl into, a place with cool soil and leaves, safe in the shadows of whispering trees. Like under those trees right there at the far end of that field.

What was that? Under the trees, the shadows shifted slightly. In the dark, something darker still. It moved again. Coins of light dappled across a black back.

A horse! A black horse!

The horse of her dreams.

As the bus rumbled along, a row of trees blocked Kim's view. A white house with a silver mailbox slid by. "MacLean" stood out in clean blue letters. Kim blinked in surprise.

The MacLean farm was just down the road from her place. She'd moved from Vancouver more than ten months ago and ridden from Meadow Green to Antigonish and back again every school day since. She knew every horse and pony on that route, and she had never seen that horse before. It couldn't have been there all along.

But it was there now. A horse living almost next door. This was perfect! Things would be just like they used to be.

Just like every day of every Prince Edward Island summer for as far back as she could remember, when she and Gramma-Lou went next door to see Gramma-Lou's horses.

Well, they weren't exactly Gramma-Lou's. They belonged to Mr. Cameron, her boss. But Gramma-Lou had been looking after them forever, mucking out their stalls, grooming them and training them to race. Even after Mr. Cameron had a stroke three years ago and sold all the horses except Dan and Topper, Gramma-Lou would go over every day to help muck out and groom and, weather permitting, take each horse for a gentle jog around the track. And every day of every summer, Kim went with her.

Until last summer — because the winter before last, Gramma-Lou got so sick her doctor insisted they hire someone to look after her. Lillian, Mr. Cameron's niece, moved into the sunrise bedroom in the periwinkle blue cottage. Kim's bedroom. The one that overlooked the silken ripples of dunes and the ageless Atlantic.

Kim had to stay in the tiny airless apartment in downtown Vancouver. So did Janis, because an eleven-year-old couldn't stay home by herself.

Janis was Kim's mother. First names between friends, said Janis, who was raised in a hippie commune on Moresby Island, where everyone called everyone by their first name. She had enthusiastically weeded out "Mom" and "Dad" by the time Kim was three. Janis was like that, a nonconformist through and through. And an artist. She had been an artist all her life (and in all her past lives except when she had been a small Chinese girl who died in the influenza epidemic of 1918).

As for Colm, Kim's father, if Janis preferred first names, fine with him. As long as she looked after Kim and shipped her off to Gramma-Lou's every summer so Janis and he could go on his annual research expedition into some insect-thick, boot-sucking bog to collect data on the population dynamics of his blessed orchid, *Arethusa bulbosa*.

When Kim couldn't go to PEI for the summer and Janis had to stay in Vancouver, Colm went into a rage.

Summer was their special time, he ranted. Camping was no fun alone. Who was going to cook? Who was going to keep him warm at night? His mother couldn't be *that* sick. Kim could look after her. That Cameron woman was sucking up all of Lou's life savings. He had plans for that money. Everything was ruined. It was all his mother's fault.

Everything was always his mother's fault ... or Kim's.

By the end of June, Colm had finally shut up and gone off to a bog in Nova Scotia by himself.

But that was last year. Now they were all living in Nova Scotia, and Gramma-Lou was coming to stay. And Kim had just discovered a horse almost next door — she didn't have to worry about her grandmother leaving Dan and Topper behind. They could go visit the black horse every day. It was perfect!

All Kim had to do was get permission from Mrs. MacLean.

That was all. And that was impossible.

Janis had talked about Mrs. MacLean. They'd met at the Co-op grocery store. Janis said Mrs. MacLean grew up with Gramma-Lou and was very interesting. Kim knew "interesting" was another word for "weird." Just like Janis, who could talk to anyone, anywhere, anytime. The complete opposite of Kim.

A blackness as dark as Mrs. MacLean's horse pressed at Kim. Knock on that door? Impossible. Totally, absolutely, positively — impossible.

The bus grated to a stop at a long driveway leading to an old white farmhouse. Her house. Kim jumped to her feet. She glanced down at the turquoise vinyl. The frog was gone.

A boy shouted, "Hey, Cracker Kid, where's your prince?"

Once again, every eye on the bus turned to Kim. With chin to chest, she fled.

CHAPTER 2

The Haunted House

Kim didn't stop running until the kitchen door slammed behind her. She threw her knapsack on the table and dropped into the old wooden rocker to catch her breath.

There was a horse next door! And a black horse, to boot! How was she ever going to get to see it? With Janis in PEI helping Gramma-Lou pack, there was no one to ask Mrs. MacLean.

Talking to strangers terrified Kim, especially when talking about horses. She got so nervous and so excited that she shivered and stammered and made a total fool of herself. Even if by some miracle she *could* talk to Mrs. MacLean, the woman would just think she was one more annoying kid begging for a free horseback ride. She'd see how desperate Kim was, how pathetically horse crazy. She'd laugh.

"I can't do it!" Kim shouted to the house.

The butter yellow walls remained calm, soothing, like summer sunshine, summer smiles. But what about Gramma-

Lou? the walls reminded. Don't forget Gramma-Lou.

Darn it. Why did Janis paint the kitchen the exact same color as Gramma-Lou's kitchen? Even without the yellow paint, the house made her think of Gramma-Lou almost every day. After all, Gramma-Lou had lived in it as a little girl.

The first time Kim had heard about the house was the February before last, when they were still living in Vancouver. Colm returned from his job interview in Nova Scotia bouncing around like a four-year-old overdosed on sugar. He'd got the job — his first tenure-track position! No more being a sabbatical-leave replacement! No more moving every year! But Janis interrupted: how did he know he had the job when the university wasn't going to decide for another month?

Colm gloated and said he had something the other applicants didn't have. He puffed up his narrow 6'4" frame, poked out his bearded chin and counted off on his fingers in that big dramatic way of his. "They were looking for a botanist or a geneticist — can't beat my PhD in plant genetics. Then there's my eleven years' teaching experience, twelve years of research, the armload of published papers and ..." He giggled and rubbed his hands together, "... and ROOTS! That's what they like down there. Roots. History. 'What's your father's name?' That sort of thing."

Janis looked as confused as Kim felt.

Colm rolled his eyes. "Use your brains! My mother grew up in Meadow Green! Twenty minutes from the university! You should have seen the look on the dean's face when I told him. And ..." He paused again.

"And what?" Janis asked impatiently.

"And I told him I was buying the very house my mother grew up in. Put down a deposit on it yesterday."

Kim's heart skipped a beat. "We're going to live in Gramma-Lou's house?"

"A deposit? On a house?" Janis gasped. "We don't have that kind of money! You told me just last week you had to cut back on my allowance."

Colm's good mood vanished. "I was giving you too much."

"How could it be too much? The only place Kim and I can shop is the thrift store."

"You could buy new clothes if you didn't spend so much on gas. Do you think I can't read an odometer? Do you think I don't know how much you drive?"

"But I have to run errands, get groceries."

"Where the hell's the grocery store? Alberta? I'm not working my ass off so you can drive all over creation. I'm going to sell that car. You can take the goddamn bus."

"But ... I need to do research for my paintings ... get out of the city. See the forest up close. See rare plants. Take some pictures."

The zigzag scar on Colm's left cheekbone glared white against his sudden redness. He grabbed a *National Geographic* and threw it at Janis. "Use pictures in there for your stupid paintings."

"My paintings aren't stupid!" Janis looked like she was going to cry. Instead she stamped her foot and shouted, "Your plants are stupid!"

"At least my plants are alive!" Colm bellowed. "Your

paintings are dead. Only some depressed suicidal maniac would buy one of those ugly things."

Kim put a protective hand on Janis's arm and scowled at Colm. He knew Janis poured her heart into her paintings. He should never have said that — even if it was true.

Janis's paintings weren't pretty. Over the years, they had gotten more and more detailed and more and more lifeless — intricate, lifeless landscapes. But Colm had never attacked Janis's work like that before. He and Kim would be eating Kraft Dinner for a month.

Janis didn't burst into tears, or shrivel into a numb silence, or run away. Not that day. That day Janis took a deep, shaky breath and said, "Maybe you'd be happier if I took Kim and went back to Moresby. That would save you money."

Kim couldn't believe her ears! And Janis sounded like she meant it.

Janis had never gone back to Moresby Island since she had run away to marry Colm. Kim had heard about the beautiful Queen Charlottes on the BC coast only from school and television. Rain forests and mountains and totem poles of the Haida Gwaii. She smiled.

Colm slammed his fist on the wall. "You said you hated that place! You said you wanted adventure and travel. I gave you that. We've been from Mexico to Alaska. Now you say you'd rather go back to that island and share some hut with twenty brain-dead hippies? You go right ahead. Never mind I bought you the perfect house in the country. Never mind it has an enormous painting studio you can have all to yourself."

"A studio?" Janis murmured. She chewed her lip. "But we can't afford a house."

"Wrong. Wrong. Wrong. It was dirt cheap. The mortgage payments will be less than the rent on this hole."

"But a house, Colm. You should have talked to me first."

"There wasn't time. The minute I gave the real estate agent my deposit, the seller called up and tried to talk me out of it. He said he knew who my mother was and gave me some crap about this guy everyone calls Crackers who owned the place ages ago and went crazy and shot himself or something. He even tried to convince me that Crackers was my grandfather. Idiot!"

"Gramma-Lou's father's name was Crackers? And he killed himself?" Kim exclaimed.

"Of course not! His name was Fred," Colm growled.

"He died in Halifax, Kim," said Janis. "Colm, why on earth would the man tell you a story like that?"

"Isn't it obvious? He got a better offer from someone else. How stupid does he think I am? Telling me some cockamamy story about the house being haunted."

"Gramma-Lou's house is haunted?" asked Kim.

"It's not your grandmother's house," Colm snapped. "She hasn't lived there for fifty years. It's *my* house. And of course it's not haunted. Use your brain. There's no such thing as ghosts."

"But why would he say that?" asked Janis.

"What the hell does it matter? The deal is done and that's that." Colm turned on the TV, signaling there would be no more talking.

A month later, Colm officially got the job, and in

August they moved to Nova Scotia. Janis remained tense. What if she didn't like the house? What if it really was haunted? She had fretted all the way from Vancouver to Antigonish. It had been a very long drive.

But the moment Janis saw the studio built off one side of the house, with its large north windows and its door with a lock, she couldn't stop smiling. She immediately set about unpacking her paintings and supplies — and telling Kim that the house wasn't haunted or she would have felt it. Remember her séance leader in Vancouver had said she was very receptive? Hadn't she been able to communicate with her dead parents?

Kim didn't care. She loved the house before she even saw it. It had once been Gramma-Lou's house. And when Kim did see it, she loved it even more. It stood solidly in the middle of a strip of land with a lawn out front so big it took Colm two hours to mow. Behind the house was a barn, a gigantic elm tree and four acres of fields that rolled down to meet the alders creeping up from the Pomquet River.

The house was huge. It had more rooms than the three of them could clutter — even Colm, the Master of Mess, who never picked anything up or put anything away. Every horizontal surface collected the debris of his laziness. Since they had arrived, the empty bedrooms had steadily accumulated papers and books and tools and towels and dust and dead flies, along with the mountain of boxes he had hauled from Vancouver.

Every time they moved — more boxes. Colm refused to throw anything out. He'd go through them when he got time, he said. He never got time. For this last move, they had to rent an extra-large U-Haul. Janis kept insisting he leave some stuff behind, but Colm tightened his jaw and muttered words like "important," "essential," "critical." To Kim, the word that came to mind was "bonfire."

In the Vancouver apartment, cartons were stacked behind the sofa, under tables and all the way up the hall wall — a good sound barrier against the neighbors shouting at Colm to stop shouting. At least now his collection was out of sight — out of sight, out of mind.

Neither Colm nor Janis mentioned Crackers again, so Kim figured Colm must have been right about the previous owner making it up. Until the day she started school.

News of where she lived spread faster than the measles in a daycare. Every kid, from the curious to the plain nasty, asked her stupid questions like, "What's the ghost look like?" "How do you sleep in a haunted house?" "Does blood really drip from the ceiling?" "Does the river turn red when it rains?" And they all called her Cracker Kid. It was beyond horrible.

Kim started to believe the story about Crackers shooting himself. And why not? Dramatic deaths ran in her family. Janis's parents died in a boating accident while trying to rescue a killer whale. And Colm's father threw himself off a thirteen-story scaffold the day his divorce papers went through. (That's what Gramma-Lou said. Colm said his dad fell.) And Gramma-Lou's older sister, Lynn, died when she was sixteen. Kim wasn't sure if anyone mentioned how, but sixteen is too young to die.

And then there was Janis's first cousin, Sturgis, who flew off the radar on the way to Belize. So why not a great-grandfather who shot himself?

She told Janis that the Crackers story must be true because everyone had heard about it. Janis said she'd heard a few versions of the story, too, but not to worry. "None of it is true. How could Lou's father kill himself and then sell his farm and move his family to Halifax? And your Gramma-Lou talked to me about growing up in Meadow Green. It was all good. Nothing awful happened. She should know, right?"

Then Janis reminded Kim that at least the children at school were talking to her. What a wonderful opportunity to make new friends. But it hadn't been a wonderful opportunity at all. The week before Halloween was a nightmare. The nicknames multiplied. Ghost Girl, Butcher Baby, Spook and, the worst, Cheese and Crackers, because it was often accompanied by the same squished into her hair at lunchtime. Kim stayed home sick as often as Janis could be fooled.

Finally, by mid-November, things eased off. She spent the rest of the winter in relative peace. She learned that eating lunch with the special-needs students kept the cheese and crackers at bay and, though she was tearfully lonely at least once a week, Kim liked being by herself the rest of the time, roaming the outdoors and rereading all the library's horse books.

Now the almost-summer sun spilled through the tall kitchen window, across the wide oak table and up the staircase. Kim pried off her sneakers and stuck her cold, sweaty feet into the shaft of sunlight. Her dark socks instantly soaked up the heat, but the rising fumes reminded her she was wearing three-day-old socks. The washer had been on the blink again, and it wasn't getting fixed until Janis got back from PEI.

Cripes, she missed Janis. Why had it taken three whole weeks to pack up Gramma-Lou? Janis was an experienced packer. Colm had moved to a new university every year. Kim looked at the porcelain clock on the curio shelf mounted high on the yellow wall. Janis and Gramma-Lou would be getting on the ferry any minute. They should be in Meadow Green by six at the latest. Everything was going to be perfect.

Well, almost. If she could go to Mrs. MacLean's and find out about the black horse — if it was friendly, if she and Gramma-Lou could go over and brush it every day — that would be perfect. What a surprise the horse would be for Gramma-Lou. And her grandmother would be so proud of her. Janis, too. That would be the mountaintop of perfect. But there was no use thinking like that. It wasn't going to happen. At least she still had one big surprise for Gramma-Lou. She had the ivy.

Kim thought of the pots of ivies that had lined her grandmother's dining room windowsills — masses of pointed leaves, green and silver above, deep purple-green below. She remembered how Gramma-Lou fussed over each pot, checking the soil moisture, picking off any wilted or crispy bits of leaf. She'd say, "I don't know why I keep so many," then she'd grin and pop another broken stem in a glass of water to root.

Now all the ivies were dead. Forgotten. That's what Janis had said after a brief trip to PEI last fall. Kim overheard her talking to Colm. Janis had actually turned down the television in the middle of Colm's favorite show. "All Lou's plants are dead," she had said. "She forgot to take care of them. She forgets so many things. I don't know how much longer Lillian is going to be able to handle her. We have to think about the future."

Colm never said a word. He stared at the TV for the rest of the night without turning the sound back up.

But all the ivies weren't dead. Kim had taken cuttings home with her two years ago. She now had a beautiful, flowing plant that she would present to Gramma-Lou when she arrived. Kim smiled broadly. She couldn't wait to see the look on her grandmother's face.

Kim's stomach fluttered with excitement — and hunger. She jammed her sneakers back on and went to the refrigerator. As the door sucked open, a huge white cat barreled out of nowhere. It threw its arched back against Kim's legs.

"Smudge! Where did you come from?" Kim scritched the hint of gray between the cat's ears. "Can't stay hidden when someone opens the fridge, eh?"

Smudge was Colm's cat. Colm loved cats. Almost as much as his houseplants and the old Babe Ruth baseball in the glass case on the curio shelf. He'd show them off to all visitors, after which he'd remember to say, "And this tall brunet is my wife, Janis, and the short blond one is Kim." He always pointed out how different Kim was from them — the great genetics joke Nature played on him, a geneticist. He never mentioned she looked just like his mother's side of the family.

Smudge yowled loudly as Kim took the remains of a roast chicken and a jug of orange juice out of the refrigerator. She shoved aside the pile of mail on the table and plunked down the food. Then she scraped dried strawberry jam off a knife, reached for the butter and — Kim peered at the butter dish. Fine, parallel lines etched a dainty pattern all over the rounded yellow lump.

"Yuck! Lick marks."

Smudge squinted and crouched. Kim bent down and slid the dish across the floor. "You might as well finish what you started. It's not your fault Colm forgot to put you out again." The cat hesitated for an instant, then rushed over, licking and purring noisily.

As Kim straightened up, she spied a frothy green puddle of half-digested leaves near the heating grate. "Double yuck! Cat barf. Smudge, what did you eat?"

She checked Colm's houseplants sitting, hanging and climbing on every windowsill in the kitchen, den and sunporch. They were mostly cacti with spines and prickles. Cat-proof. But the fat, juicy-leafed succulents teased Smudge constantly. And the climbing onion, pregnant onion and Egyptian onion begged to be chewed on. She didn't find any tipped pots, any broken leaves, any fresh teeth marks.

"That's strange." Then she gasped. "Gramma-Lou's ivy!"

Kim ran upstairs. "I closed the door. I closed the door." Half-certainty, half-prayer. In the upstairs hall, a trail of dirty paw prints led from her open bedroom door. Inside, Kim's ivy sprawled across the floor, the old clay pot smashed in two, soil flung out, parched white roots staring at the ceiling.

"YOU KILLED IT!"

CHAPTER 3

Lost

Kim sank to her knees. "It was the only one left."

She sobbed uncontrollably as she pinched off several limp stems. She got a glass of water from the bathroom and draped the stems over the rim. "Please let them live. Please."

A car bumped down the long driveway and stopped in the back. The car door thumped. The engine gave a last *ka-chuga ka-chuga* and was silent. Colm was home.

The kitchen door slammed. Kim wiped tears away with the heel of her hand.

"Bad cat!" Colm bellowed. "Kim? Where the hell are you? Why did you let the cat eat the chicken?"

Kim stomped down the stairs. Her father was sawing off the chunk of cat-chewed bird.

"I didn't let him!" Kim retorted. "But you let him in my room, and he killed my ivy."

"I beg your pardon," said Colm, not begging at all. "I'm positive he was out. I checked everywhere."

"I always keep my door closed. No one's allowed in there. You know that. Smudge couldn't have got in there unless you left it open."

"This is my house. I can go wherever I want."

"You left the door open. You killed my ivy."

"Look, if you want a plant in your room so bad take a piece off the climbing onion."

"I don't want one of your stupid plants. I want my ivy — Gramma-Lou's ivy. The one I grew especially for her. The one I was going to give her when she got better."

Colm stared at Kim, thin lips pursed so tightly his mustache met his beard. Smudge sat back on his hind legs and tugged the chicken chunk from his fingers.

Colm grunted. "It's not even a goddamn ivy," he said. "It's a *Tradescantia zebrina* or *Zebrina pendula*, a wandering Jew, an inch plant, but not a goddamn ivy. Use your brain."

"If Gramma-Lou calls it an ivy, it's an IVY!" Kim shouted and ran out the back door, slamming it as hard as she could.

She stood on the step, silently daring Colm to open the door. A gigantic scream coiled inside her, demanding escape. But the door stayed shut. She heard the television come on in the den. Out of sight, out of mind.

She stood there a little longer, breathing more deeply, toes uncurling, staring at the once-red barn. Rust stained half the steel roof, and the rock retaining wall along the lower side bulged a little, but the barn was solid and dry. Just inside its back door someone had built a big box stall with walls boarded nearly to the rafters and a large window looking toward the river. Aged, ankle-deep sawdust covered the plank floor, as if that someone had planned to keep an animal there and then changed their mind.

It was the perfect place to keep a horse.

But Colm had said, "No! No! No!" Colm hated horses. He had a whole ridiculous list of reasons why. Horses stink. Horses are dangerous. Horses are useless. Horses tie you down. Horses are black holes for money. And last, but certainly not least, horses ruin your life. The last time he ranted through his list, he made Kim so mad she shouted, "Horses can't be useless. Gramma-Lou said Dancing Dan's winnings paid for *your* education."

He hated that she knew that. "No daughter of mine is going to get stuck working with horses all her life! You'll go to university. You'll get a real job. Make something of yourself."

"Gramma-Lou had a real job! I want to be like Gramma-Lou."

"You'll go to university."

"You can't make me."

"Look, if you want to work from dawn till dusk, three hundred and sixty-five days a year, and never make a penny more than grocery money, then you go right ahead."

"What's wrong with that? That's what you do!"

"Don't you talk to me like that. I'm your father and I won't let horses ruin your life."

That's how the last argument had ended.

Kim jumped off the back step. "I'll show you," she growled. "There's a horse down the road, and when Gramma-Lou comes, we're going to spend every day with it. I'm going to ... I'm going to ..."

Going to what? Knock on a stranger's door and babble about some horse and get laughed at? Not this millennium. Who was she kidding? If only there was another way.

Maybe she could do it if she had another reason to knock and the subject of the horse came up "accidentally." That might work. Like if she had a kite. And it just happened to break its string and come down in the pasture. She would knock on the door and ask permission to go into the pasture to get her kite — if it was all right with the horse.

The leaves of the elm tree hung fresh and green and still. There was no wind. Not even a puff.

Dumb idea.

A dog! Maybe she could pretend she had been walking her dog and he got away and she would wander over carrying a leash, calling, "Here, Max. Where are you, Max?" That would be believable. She read that Max was the most common dog name in North America. She would ask if she could hunt the fields for her dog — if the horse didn't mind.

She had a leash. She used to walk a neighbor's Newfie all the time. But that was in the city. Country dogs ran loose. They didn't need to be walked.

There was no hope. She couldn't do it. Kim moaned at her cowardice. All she really wanted to know was if the horse was friendly and not one of those that pinned its ears back when you touched it or, worse, snapped and lifted a foot. If she knew it was nice then she could ask Janis to talk to Mrs. MacLean when she got back from PEI.

The horse wouldn't be a surprise but at least her summer could get back to normal, back to long, joyful horsey hours with Gramma-Lou.

Kim gazed toward Mrs. MacLean's, across the stretch of woods that pushed the river into a wide bend. The river! Of course! Why didn't she think of it before? It ran right behind the field where she'd seen the horse. She'd just hike along the riverbank. The heck with asking permission. She'd check out the horse without Mrs. MacLean ever seeing her. She just needed to know if it was friendly.

In her mind she saw the gravel ledge that led around the river bend to ... she let out an enormous sigh of frustration. She'd forgotten about the gaspereau trap.

Kim first saw the trap when Colm had invited her to help him catalog the plants along the riverbank. It was late August. Colm was in a good mood. He had a new job, a new house and new flora to catalog. She had enjoyed that day. When she spotted a feral *Euonymus europaeus*, Colm said she had a good eye.

Downriver from their place, they came upon the permanent fencelike structure running a third of the way across the water. Colm told her it was a gaspereau trap. He said when the fish swam upstream in June to spawn, fishermen put a huge mesh-covered box at the end of the fence, and fish would get funneled into it. Then they were hoisted from the water, pickled in salt and shipped to Barbados. During the off season, the box was hauled out of the river, well out of reach of winter ice.

Two weeks ago, Kim noticed the mesh box had been hauled back into the river. An old puke green pickup loaded with barrels came and went almost daily along Mrs. MacLean's road. The gaspereau were swimming upstream and at least two men were working the trap. Two strangers.

So much for the river. She'd have to go through the woods. Kim looked at the wide band of tall ash trees up to their waist in alders. If she kept the sun a little over her right shoulder, she could walk in a straight line through the woods, across the little road that led to the fish fence, through woods again, right to where the river met the back of Mrs. MacLean's property. No problem. She had gone walking in woods lots of times with Gramma-Lou.

Kim walked to the edge of the field, where the grasses gave way to partridge berry and fern and alder trees. Each tree was actually a clump of narrow, twisted trunks holding up umbrellas of crooked branches. Kim wove between the trees, keeping pretty well on course. Gramma-Lou had taught her how to find north by the moss that grew on the north side of the older trunks and how to tell the difference between moss and the gray-green lung lichen that grew on any side of a tree.

That was the kind of stuff she'd thought she'd learn last year from Girl Guides — what wild plants you could eat, how to build a shelter, how to find your way with a compass. But the other girls couldn't find their way through an exit sign. They only wanted to go to the mall, paint their toenails and read teen magazines.

The ground beneath the alders softened. Musty dampness seeped through the sides of Kim's sneakers. She spied a small animal trail, maybe used by rabbits or deer.

On PEI, she'd seen deer vanish into what seemed like impenetrable bush only to discover a tiny path when she looked hard enough. She followed the trail, ducking often to deer height. Twice she had to scale wind-toppled trunks bristling with sharp shattered branches that any deer could have bounced over in a blink. Still, Kim figured the route was easier than cutting straight through the woods, and she could tell it ran generally southwest, from the direction of the sunlight sparkling through the dark green ceiling.

Mature ash trees seemed to mark bends in the route, and three times other paths crossed the one she followed. She came upon a clump of maple trees with trunks folded by some long-since rotted-away fallen trunk that had left each maple with a knee and lap, like chairs for forest elves. Kim perched on one to rest her back, tired from stooping under the knotted growth, trying not to get beetles in her hair. The tiny iridescent sapphire bugs clung to the alder leaves by the dozen. They chewed out the green bits, leaving nothing but brown lacework skeletons. It would have been quite beautiful if the beetles hadn't kept jumping into her hair.

"I must be almost there," she told the twisted trees. But she really wasn't sure. Like Gramma-Lou often said, "Going is always slower than coming."

Kim ducked under old clumps of leaning trunks and abruptly faced a wall of young trees so dense she could barely squeeze between them. She pushed on for another twenty steps, expecting to find more open growth. A bird song buzzed almost in her ear, but its maker was invisible in the thicket of twigs and leaves. Thin, whippy branches snagged her shirt. One sprung back and slapped her across the cheek. She choked back tears. She couldn't keep on course in here. No direct sunlight penetrated the dense growth. No moss clung to the narrow trunks. No way was she getting to Mrs. MacLean's pasture through these woods.

She headed back the way she'd come. It seemed farther than before. Farther than it should be. An uncomfortable flutter started in Kim's stomach. Mud crawled into her socks. Hard, dead twigs scratched her arms. Much farther than it should be. She could find no trees with knees. No trails. She was lost.

Panic pressed at her throat. Sweat poured down her spine. "No. You can't get lost this close to home."

She tried to retrace her footsteps to the dense thicket and head for home in a slightly different direction. She looked at her watch. After five. Well after. Gramma-Lou would be arriving soon. Kim put her arms over her face and plowed through a tangle of branches.

"Where the hell is that path?" she demanded.

An ovenbird shrilled in reply, "Not here, not here, not here."

Kim sucked in a breath, almost a sob. She stopped and stared at the swirls of mud wicking off her sneakers and into the thicket. Brown ribbons flowing ever so slowly away. Flowing downhill. Flowing to the river.

Relief washed through her. "Of course! Go with the flow."

She followed the mud through the trees. Almost

immediately the alder growth thinned, brightened and opened onto the wide graveled riverbank — right in front of the fish trap.

Kim froze, glanced left, right, up the narrow road. No sign of anyone. She'd struggled through the woods for nothing. She kicked a rock. It skittered away, bouncing off the wooden slats of the fence and onto a pile of dead fish. A buzz of flies jumped into the air. An annoyed seagull screamed overhead. Six more sat on the opposite bank, waiting to finish their meal. The dead fish stared up at Kim, the ones that still had eyes, chunks of flesh ripped from their silver-plated sides. A gust swirled the stench in her direction. Pinching her nose, she rushed past, dragging the stink in her wake like an ugly, clingy fart.

She hurried home along the riverbank, where local kids on four-wheelers had pressed rutty tracks through the tall weeds and stones. When she got to her property, Kim ducked under some blackberry canes and onto the narrow footpath worn deep by more than a century of use. She jogged along the path to the field.

Janis's car wasn't behind the house. The boat must have been late. Or they missed it. Kim ran inside to ask Colm when they were coming. The house was quiet except for the growling of the refrigerator and a steady, wheezing snore from the den. The TV was off, and Colm was fast asleep.

Kim remembered the last time Gramma-Lou came to visit. They were living in Toronto that year. Kim was seven. Gramma-Lou flew up to bring Kim back to PEI.

Their flight got canceled, and Gramma-Lou had to spend the night. The whole time, Colm had been as uptight as a thirty-five-car pileup.

This evening, Colm was sleeping like a baby. Gramma-Lou couldn't be coming any time soon.

Kim wanted desperately to ask Colm what had happened, but she knew better than to wake him.

She tried to fill her emptiness with leftovers. She took no care to be quiet, rattling pots and plates and utensils. The snoring continued unabated.

She spread out a newspaper on the table while she ate and concentrated intensely on the classifieds — section 244 — "Horses and Equipment."

A new ad read "16hh gr. QHxT g, 5 yr, green broke w/t/c, jump prospect, $3000 obo." That probably meant a sixteen-hand-tall, gray, half-quarter horse, half thoroughbred gelding, five years old, just started being ridden, has done walk, trot and canter at least once under saddle, might make a good jumper some day, for three thousand dollars, or best offer. Most ads used "TB" for thoroughbred. Maybe it was another breed that started with the letter T. Maybe Trakehner? She saw that breed advertised a couple of times, though the ads usually said "Trak" and had huge price tags. Trakehners were from Europe, and the European breeds cost all outdoors. So at three thousand dollars, the T in this ad probably meant thoroughbred.

She puzzled through the ads in the couple of dozen other newspapers she found dropped around the kitchen. By nine o'clock, her last wisp of hope vanished with the light outside. Janis never drove after dark. Gramma-Lou was not going to arrive in Meadow Green tonight, and that was final.

Kim wrote a note to Colm — "When is G-L coming?" Then she made up another plate of leftovers, covered it with plastic, taped the note on top and placed it in the fridge. She arranged the mail on the table into a large arrow of envelopes pointing Colm to his supper and her note.

She went upstairs and took her time in the shower, carefully picking flakes of bark from her long, tangled hair. Then she rushed into her room and got into her flannelette nightie and thick socks. June still cooled at night, and El Cheapo Colm refused to burn a stick of wood after May.

Perky green and purple leaves greeted Kim from the top of her dresser.

"You're alive!"

The ivy leaves were firm and full of life.

"Oh, thank you, thank you, thank you," she said to the god of small miracles.

Kim gently picked up the glass and set it where the pot had been, on the end table next to the old hand-tinted photo. "Here's your surprise, Gramma-Lou."

She spoke to the image in the dainty gilt frame, a golden-haired girl on a golden-haired horse in the middle of a sloping green field with a border of young spruce trees and a river beyond. It was ten-year-old Gramma-Lou astride Domino, a Belgian workhorse with a back so broad Gramma-Lou's legs stuck out more sideways than down.

There was no tack on the horse. Not even a halter. He

calmly posed in deep green grass while two more flaxen-maned monsters stood in the background. Gramma-Lou had told Kim how she'd push Domino over to the fence and he'd stand perfectly still while she climbed aboard. Then they'd wander around the pasture, sometimes for hours, while he grazed. Sometimes she'd grab a fistful of blond mane and bump him with her heels and he'd trot gentle circles around his friends, Stacey and Sue. Sometimes she'd lie back and watch the swallows dance overhead. Sometimes she'd even fall asleep.

The photo was taken the year before her father sold the farm and all the animals and moved the family to Halifax. The year before Gramma-Lou said good-bye to Domino forever. She told Kim no matter how much she loved the standardbreds she worked with as an adult, Domino was always dearest to her heart. She still missed him.

Kim touched the smile in the photo. "I miss you, Gramma-Lou."

She shivered and dove under the blankets. Despite Gramma-Lou's old saying "The sooner asleep, the sooner tomorrow comes," Kim was in no hurry to go to sleep. The sooner asleep, the sooner dreams come.

The dreams were getting worse lately — tiny nightmares now. They'd started not long after moving to Meadow Green. Odd snippets of damp darkness. Every night the same thing. They lasted only moments, like a shout that startles you awake then leaves you wondering if you heard anything at all.

She'd learned to ignore them pretty well, but lately the bursts of darkness were resolving into images that rippled and dodged like creatures moving behind a curtain of flowing water. Kim had tried to go toward them, but fear would force her awake.

The dreams didn't make any sense. Weren't dreams made of things picked up during the day, a word here, an image there, all colliding and sorting as she slept? Where did they come from? Gramma-Lou said she was sensitive to things others missed, so that must be it.

Kim still didn't feel any better about falling asleep. She wished she had a new book to read. She thumbed through a few horse magazines that Janis had bought her, but it was no use. She was too exhausted and distracted to focus on the words. She yawned for the hundredth time. "Good night, Gramma-Lou," she finally said to the photo. "Hurry home." And she fell asleep.

She knew she was dreaming. She clenched herself, waiting for the shout of darkness. Instead she dreamed a world of rain, and through it she saw the horse, not black but golden, and he was looking straight at her as the rain poured down like a million tears.

CHAPTER 4

Bus Number 36

Kim awoke with dried tears on her cheeks and a sadness so deep her toenails ached. She almost preferred the scary dreams to that one.

The house was empty. Colm's empty supper plate sat atop the arrow of envelopes, next to a dirty cereal bowl. On her note he had scrawled "Maybe next week — J will call Fri at 6."

Next week! Why next week? It wasn't fair. And she couldn't talk to Janis until tomorrow night! Colm and his stupid long-distance bills. It wasn't fair.

She should have gone to PEI with Janis. She could pack better and faster than Janis ever could. She should be with Gramma-Lou right now, sitting cross-legged on the crocheted cushions, eating homemade blackberry jelly on molasses bread, with the sunlight reflecting off the yellow walls and Gramma-Lou's smile. She should be putting on her red-toed black rubber boots and walking hand in hand to the Camerons' barn, to the sinus-clearing scent of liniment, creosote and ammonia, to the two rugged horses nickering noisily for their turn to tear up the track, kicking gravel at Gramma-Lou's goggles.

And this afternoon she and Gramma-Lou should be shouldering knapsacks and going hiking deep in the forest, enclosed in leaf curtains and bird songs, or down along the endless beach, where the cool salt winds rose, or up into the dunes, where they'd build a bonfire and roast and re-roast marshmallows until nothing remained but sticky driftwood branches, flickering embers and full hearts.

Instead Kim forced down three half-warmed frozen waffles, glad she didn't have to make Colm his porridge and risk missing the bus. She got to the roadside fifteen minutes early and patiently waited. For number 36 — the Bus from Hell.

It was the school-bus driver's fault. He hated kids. That's what everyone said, and Kim was inclined to agree. One morning she was only twenty steps from the road when he slammed the door and left. It was like he didn't see her. And how could he? He never looked past the bus steps. He just pulled up, opened the door, counted silently to six, closed the door and drove off. If there were more than two kids at the bus stop, they'd have to run aboard or the slowest would get smacked by the door. Or left behind. It was the same at every pickup. Stop, open, six-count, close, leave. Even when there was no one waiting.

Maybe he hoped someone would get off.

The bus driver hated kids, and the kids hated the bus driver. Especially the little kids, and the geeks and brains and quiet ones who sat near the front, trying to study —

or simply survive the journey. They hated him because he set no rules. No one ever got punished by being put in the front seat or reported to the principal or suspended from riding the bus. The back-seat bullies could fight and steal lunches and hurl food and spitballs and dirty words, and the bus driver never took his eyes off the road. He never defended the kids being pelted with peanut butter or dripping wads of paper pulp — or cheese and crackers. He just crammed his hat down to his bushy red eyebrows and drove.

Today, as usual, the bus roared up on time. The door opened. Kim climbed aboard. Normally she would rush to sit down before the old beast of a bus lurched forward and knocked her over. Normally she'd keep her eyes on the floor, grab the first free seat and concentrate on the scenery until the bus pulled off the highway and headed for the school. Then she'd fixed her gaze on the door, ready to run for it. There was always at least one stolen peanut butter or cheese snack left to be squished into the hair of a straggler.

Today wasn't normal. There was a horse at Mrs. MacLean's, and Kim needed to see it. Her usual seat looked out the wrong side of the bus. She had to find a different seat. She had to look up, scan faces, risk eye contact. She shot a fleeting glance down the aisle. The bus was barely half full. All the MacLean-side seats were occupied except for one just behind the arrows — the big black arrows painted halfway down the sides, directing you out the rear door in case of emergency. Only big kids sat behind the arrows. Cool kids. The ones the back-seaters rarely messed with.

Kim absorbed all this in three heartbeats. The bus grated and groaned. She bolted for the seat. Too late. The bus jumped forward, pitching Kim off her feet. She grabbed the seat back as she fell past, twisted her shoulders hard, using her momentum to execute a perfect 180. She hit the vinyl with a solid smack, startling the boy in the seat behind. The book on his lap fell to the floor.

"Hey!" he barked.

Hot embarrassment flooded past Kim's collar and up to her eyebrows. Big mistake, she moaned to herself. Leave now. But her legs had turned liquid.

She heard the boy say, "That's okay, Shrimp. Thought you were one of those brain-deads from down the road. Will you pass me my book?"

His voice was calm and friendly. She fished under her seat for the book and held it up over her shoulder. Out of the corner of her eye, she saw an illustration of a rearing horse on the cover.

"Thanks," he said.

The bus bumped past the cornfield pinstriped with ankle-high sprouts, past blocks of half-tall hay and pastures dusted with dandelions. Then it looped away from the river to the valley edge, where wooded hills lay quietly, like thick green quilts tucked around sleeping giants. Then back again toward the river and Mrs. MacLean's.

Kim peered into every shadow of every tree as they drove by. Was that the horse or just her imagination? She couldn't say. The house blocked her view and then some trees, and then they pulled up to the next stop.

Slug's stop.

Three boys stomped on. Slug, the meanest eighth-grader on the planet, shoved a younger boy down the aisle, probably his brother — they both wore unlaced work boots and smelled like armpits.

"Am too getting a four-wheeler," Slug said.

"With what? The only thing you got that's worth shit is your dumb collection of old baseball cards," his brother said. "They ain't gonna buy a quad."

Slug shoved him again. "No, asshole. With the money Dad owes me."

"You're nuts. He'll never give it to you."

"Already has. He just doesn't know it yet." Slug strolled to the back seat, staring menacingly at every kid he passed.

The third boy to board the bus balanced expertly against the acceleration and stopped beside Kim. "Vamoose, Squirt," he ordered.

Kim was too terrified to move. For some stupid reason, it had just occurred to her that sitting one seat behind the arrows meant only three seats in front of the back seat — Slug's seat. Too close! Way too close!

How stupid could she be? She had to get out of there. Before he spotted her. Before he did something humiliating and laughed his ugly dark laugh. Before he demonstrated once again how he had turned the nickname Cracker Kid into Cheese and Crackers and made it stick in more ways than one.

Her head felt swimmy. The boy behind her said to the boy in the aisle, "Hey, Mike. Sell any chocolate bars yet?"

"Nah," said Mike, slipping into the seat next to him.

Kim hunkered down in misery. The bus pounded over the potholes, drumming out "Too close ... too close ... too, too, too close." She tried escaping to the back of one of her imaginary horses, but the forest crowded into the ditch — no place for her to run.

Keeping her peripheral vision alert for flying objects, she focused on her knapsack. She began counting the number of stitches along the flap. Twenty-one, twenty-two ... Big mistake. Her stomach rolled over and greenness pushed up her throat. She clamped her eyes shut. Way better to get hit by peanut butter than to puke.

There was absolutely nothing worse than puking. Not getting a "Kick me" sign stuck on your back, or discovering in third period your T-shirt is inside out, or being accused of copying Abby's test when it was the other way around, or even fainting in class. No, there was absolutely nothing worse than puking — except puking in public.

Kim never could focus inside a moving vehicle without getting sick. She always wondered how kids read on the bus. The boy behind her could do it. She knew without opening her eyes that he was reading. She heard him turn a page. Strange how she could hear that — how quiet it was on the bus today.

The bus squealed to a halt, paused, lurched forward, again and again, hauling its load toward town. Inside, the bizarre silence continued. The only sounds over the growling motor were some sniffing and coughing. Even the back seat was weirdly silent. She should have found it a pleasant change, but it was too strange ... and scary, definitely scary. Like the calm before the storm.

And then she heard it. They all heard it. The forceful puff of air from the back seat, followed by the solid, splattering smack against the front windshield.

Everyone looked up with a collective sputter of astonishment. There it was, dead center of the glass, the biggest, drippiest, most disgusting spitball in the history of spitballs, sliding slowly toward the dash.

Kim couldn't decide what was more amazing: the monstrous size of the spitball, the impossible distance it had traveled or the bus driver never so much as twitching. He just negotiated the next intersection as if a mouthful of chewed pulp and slime was a normal part of the view.

Then the second one hit. Right on the mirror in front of the driver's head — the mirror designed so the driver can keep an eye on the kids. The mirror *this* driver never used.

"Gross!"

"How much paper in one of those?"

"Historic!"

"How'd he do that?"

"Disgusting!"

"What kind of cannon did he use?"

"No wonder he was so quiet."

Chaos returned. All manner of things started flying through the air.

Kim slouched to her smallest, hugging her knapsack and praying to the god of grandmothers to spare her.

"Hey, Shrimp, I'm talking to you."

Something nudged her knee. She opened her eyes.

The boy with the horse book was sitting beside her,

his knees poking dents in the seat ahead. On his feet were huge black and white sneakers, expensive and well worn. He balanced a smallish cardboard carton on his lap.

"You didn't really think you'd get warts, did you?"

Kim squished tight to the side of the bus. No one ever sat beside her on purpose.

"Warts," he repeated.

It was the first time anyone had ever called her that.

"From yesterday's frog." He shrugged. "So, like I said, are you going to sell chocolate bars, or what?"

Kim stared at the floor, waiting for him to go away.

"Come on. I know you're only in grade six, but you're the only one living on this stretch of road. And it's for a good cause. You just have to take a few bars. Everybody needs a chocolate fix. Like Mrs. MacLean back there. Bet she's good for three or four bars — at least."

The name "MacLean" jolted down Kim's spine. Chocolate bars! She could go to Mrs. MacLean's with chocolate bars. She could find out about the black horse.

"You will?" said the boy.

With a shock, Kim realized she had been nodding her head. She froze. No! I can't sell chocolate bars!

"You'll take a carton, right?"

No! Wide-eyed fear forced Kim to look at him. He was a tall, skinny eighth-grader with caramel skin and hair to match. He flashed a big bright smile. "Hey, my mom bought a whole carton. That's, um ... eight to a bag, six bags to a carton, um ... forty-eight bars. She said it was the least she could do to support the Antigonish Celtic Soccer Team and," he sat up very straight, "their star player."

Kim struggled to process the idea of his mother eating that much chocolate.

The boy took her blank look as a yes. He quickly opened the carton and plunked a bag of bars on her lap.

"Start with eight."

Kim blinked at the bag.

"What's your name?"

When Kim didn't respond, the boy twisted his head and read the name black-markered on her knapsack. "Kim O'Connor. Hi, I'm Tim Ritland. Kim ... Tim. Hey, we rhyme."

The bus turned off the highway at the traffic lights. "Only in Antigonish," said Tim, babbling on. "Did you know that? Of course with this third set of lights up here, the old joke shifts a bit. Used to be if you wanted to give directions to Antigonish to anyone in Canada you'd tell them to get on the Trans-Canada and drive east until they hit the traffic lights and then turn left. Now they'll end up at our school. Cool, eh?"

Still no response. Tim shrugged his bony shoulders.

Kim gathered for the dash to the door as the bus pulled into the school yard. She started to stand and then realized with despair that there was no quick way past Tim's long legs.

Tim grabbed her T-shirt and yanked her back down. "Stay put!" he hissed. "Slug will think you're afraid of him."

I am! I'm doomed!

The bus stopped. Kids plowed to the exit. Slug started down the aisle, herding the frightened pack with a steady stream of tiny, well-aimed spitballs. He paused beside Kim's seat.

Her heart stopped.

Tim rose and squared his shoulders.

"Humph," grunted Slug and re-aimed his shooter at the heads by the door.

"You can move now, Shrimp," said Tim.

Kim's heart started beating again. Only she and Tim were left on the bus! She stuffed the bars into her knapsack and walked behind him to the door. Tim met up with Mike and a boy in loose-fitting skater clothes. The three headed across the school yard.

Tim suddenly turned and shouted, "Kim, I forgot! They're two bucks each!"

Kim blanched as heads turned her way. The boys with Tim said something and laughed. Kim couldn't make out their words — her pulse pounded too loudly in her ears.

She spent the rest of the school day in an agony of hope. Maybe she could do it. Yes, maybe she *could* sell chocolate bars to Mrs. MacLean.

CHAPTER 5

Door to Door

The bus ride home was uneventful. Slug wasn't on board. Neither was Tim. No one bothered her.

Kim thought she saw the horse under the trees at Mrs. MacLean's again but wasn't sure. A confusion of sunlight and shadows frolicked in the wind.

At home she tossed her knapsack on the table and pulled out the bag of chocolate bars, her tentative resolve crumbling. "What's the use?" she asked the house.

"Talking to yourself is the first sign of insanity," said Colm from the den door. He gave Kim such a start she squealed. Colm chuckled. "What's the use of what?"

"What are you doing home?"

"Power failure. No fume hoods, no labs. Stupid rules. It's only ten percent formalin. People have used it forever without fume hoods. Never hurt me. Yum, what do we have here?" He fished into the bag of chocolate bars.

"Don't touch those!"

"I want one."

"NO!"

"Why the heck did you bring them home?"

"I'm going to sell them to Mrs. MacLean."

"Ha, when hell freezes over." He took out a bar.

"No!" Kim jerked the bar from Colm's hand, grabbed the bag and marched out the door.

There was no turning back now. Up the driveway she marched. She headed toward town, walking atop the ridge of loose gravel pushed to the side by passing tires.

A fresh breeze kept the cloud of blackflies behind her. Anxiety grew with each step. "You can do this," she lectured herself. "It's for a good cause." She smirked at her twist of Tim's phrase. Her cause wasn't soccer. It was Gramma-Lou. And the black horse.

Kim could picture the horse in front of her, her hand sliding along his satin coat. She hadn't touched a horse since her last trip to PEI. Unless she counted Queenie. But Queenie was a pony, and though ponies were cute and huggable, a horse made her heart race in the very best way. When she touched one, breathed one, everything was right in the universe.

She had to admit, though, Queenie had been pretty special. She met her last October — the last time Janis went "exploring." That's what Janis called it, but Kim knew running when she saw it.

A day or two after a particularly bad fight with Colm, Janis would pack Kim and a suitcase into the car and drive. More than once, Kim wondered if they'd go home again, and more than once she said she wished they wouldn't.

47

"Why are we going back?" she'd asked.

Janis would simply answer, "Tomorrow will be better."

Sometimes on those explorations, if they saw a pony in a field or a backyard, Janis would slow the car. Every time, Kim nearly died of hope ... and terror. Hope that Janis would turn up the pony's driveway. Terror that Janis would turn up the pony's driveway.

That October, Janis drove up a driveway in Roman Valley, parked the car and said as she always said, "Now be brave and go ask if you can see the pony." And, as always, no matter how much Kim wanted to see that pony up close, fear glued her to her seat.

"They won't let me see it."

"How do you know that?"

"I just know."

"Knowing isn't enough," said Janis. "It's doing that counts. That's what your grandmother always says. She's a doer. Be a doer like her." Janis had that bright, fierce look in her eyes she always got when she spoke about her mother-in-law. The same look she got each time she put the suitcase in the car.

When Kim didn't budge, Janis dragged her out of the car. "A woman has to be strong."

"I'm only twelve!"

Janis dragged her to the door, knocked and asked the lady who answered if her daughter could see the pretty pony. The lady said "Of course you can" in that Nova Scotian welcome-the-world-into-your-kitchen kind of way. That's when Janis asked how big the pony was going to grow. Kim shriveled in embarrassment. Hadn't she told

Janis a million times that ponies weren't baby horses?

The lady was polite and said, "Queenie isn't going to get any bigger. She's almost nineteen years old." Then she commented on Janis's interesting vest. Janis took it as a compliment and talked about how she had sewn it out of pieces of old sweaters she'd gotten from the Opportunity Shop. And then she just kept on talking. Janis could talk to strangers like nobody's business. And tell them everything. Nothing was private. Kim hated it.

But she really liked Queenie. She was white and wide, with cute tippy-in ears and peaceful eyes. Kim tied a piece of rope to her halter and sat on her as she ambled around the field for twenty-five minutes. Then she gave her a long hug good-bye. She knew she'd never see Queenie again. Janis never explored the same road twice.

After talking the lady's ear off, Janis collected Kim and headed for home. On the way she made Kim change into clothes from the suitcase. "You know how Colm feels about horses. We don't want him to smell what you were up to," she had said.

Or what *you* were up to, Kim felt like saying. But she didn't because there was something different about her mother that day — like she was driving home on purpose instead of by default. Janis had changed since moving to Meadow Green. She had cut her long dark hair to short elfin feathers, exposing the butterfly tattoo on her neck. She'd paint for hours every morning and watch Oprah and Dr. Phil every afternoon. After the trip to Roman Valley, she'd settled for long chats with the cashiers and customers at the Co-op every Saturday morning, instead of strangers in the middle of nowhere. Nothing seemed to distract her from her new routine. Not even a fight with Colm.

Kim kicked a fist-sized rock into the ditch. If only Janis was here now and Kim didn't have to do this alone.

The white house with the blue door peeked through the line of spruce trees. Kim's feet glued themselves to the ground. She tried to swallow, but her mouth was too dry.

Memories flooded in. Dark memories. Selling Girl Guide cookies in Vancouver. Janis had made her join the Girl Guides. "You need friends," she had said. "Friends make you strong." Kim joined because Janis refused to take her to see the RCMP Musical Ride if she didn't.

The first Guide meeting was awful. For the second, the troop went out to sell Girl Guide cookies, but it was after supper and it was getting dark. The younger members each got paired with an older girl. Kim's partner was a sixteen-year-old named Adele. Once they were out of sight of the rest of the troop, Adele passed her cookie boxes to Kim, said "Sell these. I've got a date," and disappeared at a run. She left Kim standing alone on a doorstep on a dimly lit street in a city she barely knew. She stood there for ages, trapped between the fear of talking to a stranger and the fear of missing a once-in-a-lifetime chance to see thirty-two dancing black horses.

Finally she knocked. No one answered. She could hear them inside — laughing. At the second door, a dog snarled and tore at the mail slot with his claws. At the third, a man snarled and shut the door in her face. She rushed across the street, passing dark house after dark house. Finally a porch light greeted her and a lady took a box of cookies, went for some money ... and never came back. Kim stood on that doorstep for an eternity. She didn't know what to do. She felt sick.

Then she got lost.

Every building looked the same, every doorstep, every fence, every flowerpot. She couldn't remember which way she'd come. She remembered the smell of pizza — or was that Chinese food? Had she heard those wind chimes before? She stumbled past a corner signpost with no signs on it. A car horn hooted right beside her. The driver offered her a ride home. Kim ran — luckily, in the right direction.

She found the Guide leader's car, recognized her own jacket on the back seat. She crawled in and huddled in the dark. Car lights passed by for what seemed like hours. When the leader and the other girls returned, Kim said she felt sick. The leader asked her why she didn't just go home, in an I-don't-want-to-catch-it tone of voice. She said Kim's house was just a block and a half away. The other girls snickered as Kim shrank deeper into misery. Vancouver was so confusing, so new. Like all the other cities — always still new when she moved again.

Kim quit Guides the next day, and Janis said that was the last time she wasted what little bit of money she had signing Kim up for anything.

The memory faded into bright sunlight, hot on her back, but spasms of shivering still grabbed her. She looked at the MacLean house. This would be different, she tried to convince herself. Only one door, full daylight, green fields — and a horse.

A car approached, slowly pounding over potholes. She unglued her feet and walked on, past the lilac hedge, along the walkway and up the veranda steps. The car passed by.

The blue door loomed. Kim's feet begged to flee. But what if Mrs. MacLean had already seen her and was coming to the door?

She rang the bell.

Nothing happened. Janis had said Mrs. MacLean lived alone. Maybe she was getting deaf. Kim tried again, pressing as hard as she could. No buzzing, no bells, no chimes, no footsteps. One more try. She knocked loudly.

The door opened. Kim's blood drained to her feet. She blinked rapidly, trying to focus on the threshold. A four-footed cane stepped ahead of old leather moccasins. "Can I help you?" a soft, musical voice asked. Such a beautiful voice. Kim looked up.

Mrs. MacLean's jaw dropped. She staggered back a step and had to catch herself with her cane. "Oh, my," she said breathlessly. "You look exactly like her."

Like who? Kim wanted to ask. Her lips parted. Nothing came out.

"I'm sorry," said Mrs. MacLean. "I don't mean to be rude. Seeing you startled me so. You are the image of your grandmother's sister, Lynn, when Lynn was your age. Lou and Lynn and I grew up together, you know. I suppose Janis told you. Lynn was like an older sister to me, too." A long, uncomfortable pause held her.

She shook her head, tsk-tsking softly. "I couldn't believe it when they said Lou's son had bought the old house. Bad business that." She got that look old people get, their mind in another place, another time.

Then she sighed. "I'm sorry. Can I help you?"

"You ... you don't want to buy a chocolate bar, do you?" Kim whispered.

"Now, now. That's asking me to say no, isn't it? You should say, 'Wouldn't you just love a chocolate bar?' — with gusto. What are they in support of?"

"Um ..." Kim's brain went numb.

"I won't support any walkathons. They're a complete waste of energy. Why you children can't have a mow-athon or a pick-up-litterathon, I don't know. It's not for a walkathon, is it?"

Kim peeped, "Soccer."

"Huh? I like soccer. What position do you play?"

Kim shook her head. "No, I'm selling them for ..." She forgot his name. It rhymed with something. "Um ... Tim."

"Tall skinny boy? Big smile?"

Kim nodded. "He's their star player."

"He told you that, did he?"

Kim nodded again.

Mrs. MacLean chuckled. "Yes, that would be Tim. I'll take what you have there. How much?"

Kim vibrated with tension. She struggled to multiply eight times two dollars. Panic twisted in her gut. She had no idea how to ask about the horse before Mrs. MacLean closed the door. Through chattering teeth she said, "Um, sixteen dollars." Then, "You know Tim?" That was dumb. Of course she knew him.

"Yes. Tim grazed his pony on the river pasture last summer."

Kim was floored. It was so easy. "With the horse?" she blurted.

The old woman tensed. "What horse?"

"The one in your field."

"You saw the horse?" Mrs. MacLean walked to the edge of the veranda and looked toward the river. "My, my, my. No one's seen him in years." She was clearly talking to herself. "I wonder ... maybe with them moving back here ... and the child ... the way she looks ..."

She turned abruptly and looked at Kim. "Tell me what you saw."

Kim shivered visibly now. "Yesterday," she sputtered. "Under the trees. A big black horse."

Mrs. MacLean's eyebrows rose. "A *black* horse," she said, leaning on the word "black." "Are you sure it was black?"

Kim nodded vigorously.

The old woman's face sagged with relief ... or disappointment. Kim couldn't decide which. Mrs. MacLean tucked a strand of long gray-blond hair behind her ear. "I'm afraid you must be seeing things," she said calmly. "We've had several horses over the years and one of them *was* black. But she's gone now."

Kim fought in vain to keep from frowning. "Gone?"

"My, yes," said Mrs. MacLean. "The black horse died twenty years ago."

CHAPTER 6

The River Pasture

Kim felt as if she had been punched in the stomach. All the way home, the blackflies crowded around her head. She barely noticed. She crammed her hands into her pockets — hands that burned to stroke the warm, black coat now tumbled sixteen dollars in change over and over and over.

It made no sense. Why did Mrs. MacLean say there wasn't any horse? If there wasn't, then what was that stuff about no one seeing it in years? If she was talking about a horse that died twenty years ago, of course no one had seen it in years. So what was she babbling about? Kim kicked the gravel so hard she hurt her toes through her sneaker. There was a horse at Mrs. MacLean's. Why didn't the old lady admit it?

Gramma-Lou often told Kim she had a superb lie detector. Kim said it was easy when people lied so much. That's why she liked animals more than people. Animals never lied. And neither had Mrs. MacLean. She honestly believed there was no horse on her property.

"So what did I see? If it wasn't a horse, what the heck was it? I've seen deer and moose — it wasn't one of those. And there's no way it was a cow."

Kim sighed in frustration and re-ran Mrs. MacLean's words and the odd look on Mrs. MacLean's face when she first saw Kim — like she'd seen a ghost. Kim stopped short.

"Oh, my god! Is that what I saw? A ghost? Is that what the ghost stories are about? A ghost horse? Nah, no way. Aren't ghosts supposed to be haunted souls with unfinished business? What unfinished business could a horse have?"

Besides, the ghost stories were about Crackers and the house she lived in, not Mrs. MacLean's. And Janis had said there was no ghost.

"No, I saw a horse all right. I know a horse when I see one."

Then it hit her. It was so simple. With Mrs. MacLean needing that walking cane, she probably hadn't been near the river since forever. And that thick grove of poplar trees behind her house blocked the view. Of course!

Mrs. MacLean doesn't know there's a horse in her pasture.

A blackfly flew right into Kim's ear. She jumped, shaking her head hard and batting uselessly at the horde around her. Stay calm, ignore them, Gramma-Lou would say, they love to make you mad, more blood rushes to the skin. But Kim was anything but calm. Her face flushed hot with excitement. She was going to find that horse!

She galloped home, leaving the flies in her wake. As she burst through the kitchen door, Colm called from the den, "Kim, is that you?"

"Who else?" She barely slowed enough to make the turn to the stairs and tore up to her room. Her thoughts bounced like a day-old foal.

It must be lost — a runaway. It might not even be in Mrs. MacLean's field anymore. It might just be wandering up and down the river. Well, if it's not there when I get there, it could still come back. I can wait.

Kim dumped her knapsack out on the bed and stuffed in a blanket, a book and a flashlight. Then she closed her bedroom door tightly and ran downstairs. Loud bursts of laughter rolled out of the den. Colm always watched old cartoons before the suppertime news. It would be totally embarrassing if she ever had friends come to visit, but she never did.

She poured apple juice into an old pop bottle and shoved it into her knapsack along with a bag of chocolate chip cookies. Then she fished through the junk drawer for the least offensive-smelling fly repellent and smeared it on.

As she stepped out the back door, she paused and called back, "I'm going out for a while."

The only response came from the television — a "Meep-meep" and an explosion followed by Colm's enthusiastic chuckle. Kim closed the door.

The sun hung above the elm tree, still high in the sky for five in the afternoon. Next week was the summer solstice, the longest day of the year, the highest the sun got. Funny how the sun reached its peak at least a month before summer did. It wouldn't get really hot till the end of July.

She walked to the river worrying whether the fishermen would be at the trap. They seemed to have a screwy schedule. She'd seen their truck go by before the bus in the morning, and sometimes it would appear after supper. She decided to sneak up the riverbank until she saw the trap. If they were there, she'd try again later — or tomorrow. They couldn't fish the whole time. She prayed to the god of horses they wouldn't be there.

They weren't. Not even the dead fish and seagulls were there.

Kim crossed the little road, skirted some more alders and rounded the river bend. A neat row of tall spruce marched along the top of a low bank. The scent of lilacs drifted between the barbed wire linking each tree. Kim scrambled up the red dirt and looked over the fence.

A rectangular green field lifted gently away to a northern barrier of maples, where she had seen the horse. To her left, an ancient barn backed into the highest corner against the thick grove of poplars that ran down from the house. A small brook divided the pasture into two equal sections. In the middle, four spruce trees dangled their toes in the brook and shed cool shade on an orange-brown carpet of needles. Nice spot for a horse — but there was no horse.

She gingerly squeezed between two of the strands of barbed wire, deeply embedded in the trunks on either side, swallowed by time and still taut enough to sing a low note when Kim's knapsack plucked past. She turned right and followed the fence around the pasture. A few alders had crept under the wire at the far end and a burst of thick shrubs grew along the top near the maples. No horse there, either.

The only place left was the barn. Of course the horse was in the barn, avoiding the blackflies. Blackflies hated to go inside buildings. She jumped the brook and trotted up the slope. The barn hadn't stood up to time as well as the fence. Patches of wooden shingles and boards had been ripped off the south wall, exposing glimpses of the interior and the post-and-beam skeleton here and there. The whole structure leaned to the left, giving Kim the impression it might suddenly fold like a house of cards.

She could make out worn bales of hay slouched in the loft and some that had tumbled onto the center aisle below. She shaded her eyes against the light and peered into the shadows. Narrow stalls lined each side of the aisle, low stalls, maybe once used for cows, short cows. She stood near the opening where the large barn doors had once been, afraid to step into the leaning structure. She squinted harder into the barn's dark depths. There was a jumble of old lumber near the back. There didn't seem to be any place for a horse to hide. There was nothing living in the barn. Only swallows that swooped in and out, chittering as they passed.

Kim frowned and looked around. The fence abutted the corner of the barn. It had a tractor-wide gate, the only gate to the field. It was tied shut with an old rope.

So where did the horse go? Was there a hole in the fence? She walked the entire fence line again. Along the way she looked for the most obvious sign of a horse being around — manure. She knew in the summer bugs and flies digested a pile of manure in as little as two days, leaving behind only a spot of extra-thick, extra-green grass. The pasture was covered in extra-thick, extra-green grass. She found no manure. And the fence was solid — no sagging wire, no openings.

Kim swallowed hard, fighting back tears. Maybe the horse had jumped the fence. That must be it. It was a high fence. But the horse couldn't have just vanished into thin air.

And then she heard it. *Splash, splash, splash, splash* — the sound of hooves stepping through water.

CHAPTER 7

Questions

The sound came from the stand of spruce.

Splash, splash, splash, splash.

Had the horse been standing there all along? A shadow in the shadows? Kim walked slowly toward the brook. She couldn't see anything under the trees.

Splash, splash, splash.

Nothing at all. She halted. The breeze ruffled a spruce bough. The shadows wavered and seemed to solidify into a horse. Another gust of wind, and only shadows walked under the trees.

Splash, splash, splash.

The hair on the back of Kim's neck stood on end. Mrs. MacLean's words whispered in her mind, "No one's seen him in years." Kim let her breath out with a shudder. "A horse is a horse, after all. Even a ghost horse."

She walked into the shade of the trees and there it was.

"A *root*! Just a stupid *root*!"

A bare tree root, as thick as Kim's thumb, stuck out

over the brook. Its tip curled into the water. The current dragged the root downstream, bending it until it sprang back, slapping the surface — *splash*. Bent again, sprang back — *splash*. Bent, sprang — *splash*. Bent, sprang — *splash*.

Kim scowled at the mesmerizing movement. Of course it wasn't a ghost. How stupid could she be? She kicked a lump of mossy needles into the brook and turned for the barn, when something stopped her. Something about the ground at her feet. She crouched down and peered closely at three dents in the orange-brown carpet. Almost round dents. She placed her hand into one. Felt the deep edges with her fingertips.

"Hoofprints!" she gasped. Her mind whirled. "There *was* a horse here! I was right! So where did it go?" She sighed a determined sigh. "Well, if it was here once, it might come back."

She pulled the blanket from her knapsack, spread it on the thick grass and took out the book. It was one of her favorites, an old *Manual of Horsemanship* from the British Pony Club. Gramma-Lou had bought it at a flea market in Fortune Bay. She glanced around the field, then opened the book.

Kim knew parts off by heart, like the chapter on saddlery. When Gramma-Lou took her to a tack shop in Charlottetown three summers ago, Kim could name almost all of the items in the store. She got goose bumps just touching the saddles. She tried on a riding helmet and a black jacket with red lining. In the mirror she saw a real rider about to enter the show ring, her mount prancing under her, the crowd waiting breathlessly for her performance.

When she admired a dark brown bridle with an eggbutt snaffle bit and a red sale tag, the clerk said, "That's too big for your pony."

Gramma-Lou shocked Kim by answering, "It's just the right size." Then she bought it!

"Because you'll have a horse of your own someday," she explained later.

The bridle hung in Kim's closet. Every few months she rubbed it with the neat's-foot oil they had bought that day in the tack shop. It kept the leather from drying out and her clothes smelling like fresh leather.

Today she reread the section on conformation and "Points to look for when buying a horse." There were great illustrations of good builds and bad builds. She had learned how to analyze every horse she encountered. Most of the standardbreds were pretty well put together or they wouldn't have been able to move with speed. But there were a few odd, crooked ones that moved well despite themselves, and some of the roadside ponies Janis arranged for her to pat were great examples of bad conformation.

Kim remembered one poor pony on the outskirts of Vancouver. A scruffy little bay with a humpy roach back, over at the knee something terrible in front and cow-hocked behind. But it was sweet and leaned blissfully when she scratched it on the withers, just at the base of the mane.

It was a pretty good-sized pony, though not nearly as big as ponies got. The manual said an animal as tall as 14.2 hands was still called a pony. That meant a pony's back could be as high as she was tall. She'd never met one that tall before.

Suddenly the words "Tim grazed his pony on the river pasture last summer" popped into her head. At the time, "pony" had conjured up an image of a fat, little Shetland. Now Kim imagined that Shetland standing next to tall, skinny Tim. Not likely. Tim's pony was probably bigger. And taller. Tim's pony might even be 14.2 hands ... a small horse ... with horse-sized feet.

Like the hoofprints by the brook!

Kim shook her head. No, there was no way those prints could be a year old. And she had definitely seen a horse yesterday. She ripped open the bag of cookies, tugged the blanket around her and concentrated on her book. She would wait, and that was that.

Twenty-two pages and nine cookies later, the spruce shadows spread dark paths to the barn. Kim stretched away stiffness and looked around for the hundredth time. She was still alone except for two robins competing for best song of the evening from opposite ends of the field. The low sunlight yellowed all it touched, and lowering temperatures had cooled away the blackflies. Now it was the mosquitoes' turn to whine for their supper.

Kim looked at her watch and groaned. "Please," she prayed to the god of hopeless causes, "please bring the horse back here. I need it. Gramma-Lou needs it."

Suddenly, a bright, golden movement on the edge of her vision. She turned quickly. Nothing. Just a quiver in the golden air. Then another shift of light. Again she turned. Nothing.

She was letting her mind play tricks on her. She crammed the blanket and book into the knapsack. Where there were hoofprints, there was hope. "I'll be back tomorrow."

She walked to the river and picked a spot where the bank was the least steep. As she squeezed through the fence, a barb on the overhead wire grabbed a thin lock of her hair and ripped it out by the roots.

"Ow, ow, ow!" shouted Kim, looking up at her long blond strands snagged in the twisted barb — long blond strands mixed with even longer strands, not blond. She plucked one dark hair free and examined it closely. It was thick and heavy — from a horse's tail.

"It's black! It's from the black horse!" Then a sinking realization. "Unless it's from Tim's pony and it's a year old, like the hoofprints.

"That settles it. I have to find out more about that pony. What color is it? How big is it? I'll ask Tim tomorrow. On the bus. Just two questions. I can do that. I have to give him the chocolate bar money anyway."

She nodded firmly and hurried for home. As she approached the bend in the river, she heard men's voices over the water's chatter.

The fishermen were back. There was no going home that way. Kim trotted downriver and climbed up the bank nearer the barn. She would follow the path that led from the pasture gate up to Mrs. MacLean's and the main road. She walked quickly, invisible behind the poplar trees with their chin-high escort of unmowed root suckers. The trees stopped at the driveway. Kim's heart raced as she ducked behind the car and scurried to the lilac hedge. She hugged the thick, scented bushes all the way to the ditch. She climbed up onto the main road. She'd made it!

"Just a moment!" Mrs. MacLean shouted.

Kim froze, trapped like a deer in the headlights.

Mrs. MacLean hobbled across the lawn in her moccasin slippers. "I meant to ask you," she said, the music in her voice muted. She came up to Kim, hands pressed together chest high. "I haven't seen your mother in ages. How are her paintings coming along?"

Kim didn't have an answer. Janis hadn't let anyone in her studio since Christmas. "She's not painting now," Kim said. "She's in PEI helping my grandmother pack. Gramma-Lou's coming to live with us."

Mrs. MacLean's face filled with confusion. "To live with you? Lou?"

Kim nodded.

The old woman's eyes went wide. "No, no dear," she said. She shook her head — a vibration left and right. "No, no. That's impossible. Lou would never come back here."

~

Kim frowned all the way home. She tried to ignore what Mrs. MacLean had said. Old people often said strange things. She tried to push the words out of her head by thinking of happy things like the feel of Gramma-Lou's deep, heart-holding hugs and the sound of her laughter ringing like robins at dawn.

But Kim's frown held fast. She couldn't push away the look in Mrs. MacLean's eyes.

Only the flickering television welcomed her home. Colm was snoring on the den couch. Good. She was too tired to deal with him tonight. It was after nine but she wasn't very hungry. She nibbled on the last of the chicken and firmly decided against reheating the already overcooked vegetables. Her stomach churned from too many cookies and Mrs. MacLean's prophecy.

Kim got ready for bed. It'd been a long, long day. Falling to sleep was dead easy.

∽

The dream was crystal clear. Light shone from the door of the red barn. The huge golden horse snorted, inviting her in. Kim stepped eagerly over the threshold — into emptiness. No light, no horse — no sound but the pounding rain drowning out the screaming.

CHAPTER 8

Jelly Bean

Kim awoke with a shout, sunlight instantly bleaching the dream's darkness, leaving only an echo of screaming — a girl screaming. It wasn't Kim's voice. What did it mean? She wished Janis was home. Janis read books about dreams. Maybe she could explain it.

Colm always slept in when he wasn't teaching. Kim ate a lonely breakfast — three bowls of honey-sweetened organic cornflakes to make up for last night's skimpy supper. She got to the road moments before the bus and took her regular seat.

She rehearsed what would happen when the bus got to the school. She'd get off first. She'd give Tim the chocolate bar money as soon as he got off. He'd be pleased. He'd answer her questions — just two — "What color is your pony?" and "How tall is it?"

She was the first off the bus. So far so good. She stood near the bumper and waited. Tim appeared in the door. Say something, Kim ordered herself. He hopped down the steps. Say something now! He met up with Mike and the skater kid.

Words exploded from Kim. "I sold the chocolate bars," she said — way too loud.

The boys turned around.

Kim dug the cash out of her pocket and held it out.

Tim took it and counted. He whistled. "Sixteen dollars. You sold them all!"

Kim nodded.

"Mrs. MacLean, right?" Tim chuckled, a rippling sound like water over stones. He turned to go.

Kim sputtered, "What color is your pony?"

"Oh, cripes, not another one," said the skater.

Mike slapped Tim on the back. "Like flies to sticky paper."

"Yeah. Horseflies," said the other boy.

Tim grinned. "Told you you should trade your board for a horse."

"And a blond to boot," said Mike. "Maybe I should buy a horse."

The other boy huffed, "That's the Cracker kid, you cowpie."

"Umm, still pretty cute."

"Get yourself a board, loser. Girls dig boards."

"Yeah, I see them mobbing you."

"At least I don't smell like cow poop."

Mike took a wide swing at the skater's shoulder. The boy ducked and countered. Tim let the two take their mock battle ahead of him. He turned to Kim, head tipped cockily to one side. "So you like horses?"

Kim nodded.

"Then why don't you come see what color she is for yourself?"

The school buzzer screamed. Tim had to run to catch up with his friends. "She's just a short walk from the last bus stop," he called over his shoulder.

It was the longest Friday of Kim's life. She spent the whole day imagining what Tim's pony looked like. Part of Kim wanted it to be large and black, to settle the issue once and for all. Another part, a far bigger part, hoped to find a fuzzy little mare, white or brown or red, anything but black.

She doodled pony after pony in the margins of her notebooks. She didn't worry about the teacher calling on her. He had long since learned not to ask her questions. At each new school, at least one teacher tried to change her. Last fall, Mr. Bloomsbury was sure he could break Kim of her shyness. He insisted Kim read her essay, "How I Spent My Summer Vacation," to the class. Kim got stomach cramps just thinking about it. It was one of the worst days of her life. She stood, shaking so hard her paper went all blurry, then gray, then black.

She woke up on the couch in the teachers' lounge. Kim said she really didn't feel well, but the teacher said she had just fainted and sent her back to class. Just fainted! In front of everyone. When she got to the back door of the classroom, they all turned and stared and there was no way her feet could be forced into the room. She ran all the way to the university and told Colm she was really, really sick.

She stayed home for three days. Janis believed her lie about a sore throat. Gramma-Lou wouldn't have. Gramma-Lou had a superb lie detector, too. Not that Kim ever lied to her grandmother. Besides, Gramma-Lou knew how to make you say "ah" and check for swollen glands.

When the 2:45 buzzer sounded, Kim was the first on the bus. All the way from town, doubts sat on her excitement. She wasn't worried about needing a note to get off at a different stop. Not with this bus driver. But where was this pony? In a field in the middle of nowhere? At Tim's house? Where did Tim live? At the last bus stop? How far was the last bus stop from her house? Could she walk home?

She knew very little about Tim. He had a pony. He played soccer. His mother liked chocolate. Mrs. MacLean liked him. She imagined his pony fenced on his front lawn or tethered to an old swing set out back or kept in a converted garage or grazing loose in the ditch. No, grazing in the ditch didn't seem likely. She could tell Tim was proud of his pony. He would never let it loose to get hit by a car.

But she had seen ponies in every possible place. Well-cared-for ponies, badly neglected ponies and every-thing in between.

When the bus stopped at her driveway, a flash of panic hit her. What if, just this once, the bus driver turned around and made her get off? After six seconds, the door closed and the bus roared on. Kim started breathing again. Funny, she thought. Normally she lived in constant fear of the bus not stopping at her house. Just driving past. Taking her to god knows where.

The bus made five more stops. Still three girls left. And Tim, of course. The bus stopped beside a yellow house. The three girls piled down the steps, pushing and giggling.

"Hop to it, Shrimp," called Tim as he bounded out behind the girls.

Kim gasped. She grabbed her knapsack and leaped from the top step before the doors snapped her heels.

No one went up to the house. The three girls skipped along the road. Tim strode close behind them. Kim followed, five paces back, jogging now and then to keep up. They were above the valley, between thick forests of white spruce and balsam fir. The scent of Christmas blew through the boughs. Her lungs demanded deep breaths of the spicy-sweet air. She watched a black-and-white warbler trying to cram a green worm into a beak already overflowing with green worms. It flew over the girls and disappeared into the trees.

The road forked. Both directions looked more like driveways than roads. The left was a bit wider, a bit more traveled. The girls and Tim went right.

Did Tim live up here? Did he invite those girls to see his pony, too? Maybe they were Tim's sisters.

One of the girls was in Kim's class. Her name was Michelle. The teacher always asked her to read aloud what she'd written. Michelle wrote a lot. She looked like a writer — quiet and serious with straight mousy brown hair.

The tallest girl had short wavy brown hair and dark brown eyes. She was very pretty and knew it.

The third girl had shoulder-length blond hair and

freckles. None of them looked like Tim.

Not sisters.

The tallest girl turned and tossed Tim a very unsisterly smile. She noticed Kim and called in a loud, clear voice, "Are you going to hug a horse, too?"

Kim flinched. She'd never met anyone besides Gramma-Lou who hugged horses — or admitted it out loud. Kim would like to hug Tim's pony if it was nice and Tim didn't mind.

She shrugged.

The girls burst out laughing. Kim got that ugly sinking feeling, like they were laughing at some secret joke. Laughing at her.

It always hurt. She always managed to say something wrong or stupid or naughty without knowing it. No one ever explained. They just laughed. Kim learned never to say certain words. Mostly, she learned never to say any words.

She hung back even farther. Maybe she should turn around and go home.

Then the blond said, "They're just teasing you. We're all going to hug a horse. That's the name of the farm. Hug a Horse Farm. These brats picked on me, too, when I first came." And she gave the biggest girl a shove. The girl snorted and kicked up her heels, horselike.

"Watch out," said Michelle. "Lana kicks."

"And bites," warned Lana, her dark eyes flashing, "just like Tim's wicked pony." She pawed the air like a rearing horse and snapped her teeth at Tim.

Tim ignored her. "This is Kim," he said. "She likes horses, too. I invited her to see Jelly Bean."

The blond slowed, silently inviting Kim to catch up. "I'm Margaret," she said. "They call me Maggie 'cause I hate it. But I'm only eleven, so they get away with it." She tried to hold a frown but giggled when Lana crooned, "So sorry, Mar-gar-et."

"That's Lana," said Margaret.

Lana said firmly, "That's pronounced L-a-y-n-a. Not Lawna or Lanna — Lana!"

"And that's Michelle," said Margaret. "Be careful what you say around her or it'll end up in the school newspaper."

Michelle took no offence at the introduction. "Hi. My friends call me Mickey."

"We do not!"

"Yeah, well I wish you would," she said quietly. Then to Kim she said, "You're the Cracker kid, aren't you? So how come you fainted?"

Kim reddened.

Margaret gave Michelle a nasty look. To Kim she said, "I heard about that. That was so cool! No one ever fainted in class before. You must have been really sick. Something exotic — like scarlet fever or malaria. That's so cool."

When Kim didn't respond, Margaret went on, "I love horses, too."

"Moi aussi, j'adore les chevaux," said Michelle.

"Are you being saucy?" asked Lana.

Michelle grinned. "Moi? Oui."

Lana considered for a moment. "I like that," she said decisively.

"Tout pour vous plaire, mademoiselle."

Margaret groaned. "Enough of the French, already. We're not in school."

"Maman and Mère speak French all the time," Michelle countered.

"Yeah, if you can call what they speak in Pomquet French," said Lana. "Heck, when your mom says 'cheval' it sounds more like 'shovel,' and your grandmother sounds even weirder."

"I know how to say 'horse' in lots of languages," said Michelle. "In German it's 'Pferd.' In Italian — 'cavallo,' and Spanish — 'caballo.' All *you* can say is 'horse.'"

"Hey, Opa taught me the Dutch," Margaret said. "It's 'paard.' And I bet Lana's dad taught her how to say 'horse' in Scottish."

Lana tossed her head again. "It's not called Scottish, it's called Gaelic."

"So how do you say 'horse' in Gaelic?"

"I don't know," said Lana, annoyed.

"But your dad's from Scotland." Margaret looked at Kim. "He rolls his Rs and everything. Sometimes I can barely understand him."

"No one speaks Gaelic anymore," said Lana.

"They still speak it in Cape Breton," Michelle corrected. "I wonder how you say 'horse' in Gaelic."

Kim smiled to herself. When Mr. Cameron's horses acted up, he used lots of Gaelic words. Not words she could repeat in nice company. But she'd heard the Gaelic word for "horse" thousands of times.

"'Eoch' or 'each,'" she whispered.

"She speaks!" Lana crowed.

"You know Gaelic?" asked Michelle.

Tim interrupted. "Come on, babies. Can't you walk and talk at the same time? There are chores to do." And he strode on ahead.

Lana's eyes flashed. "Who are you calling babies?" she shouted to his back. "I'm a D2 Pony Clubber, and don't you forget it. The others are babies."

"Especially me," sighed Margaret. "I'll never pass the D test this year if my mom doesn't buy me a Pony Club manual."

"I have one." Kim found herself speaking again.

"Do you have the eleventh edition?" asked Lana. "I have the eleventh edition."

Kim reddened again. Margaret positioned herself slightly between Kim and Lana. "Having any edition is better than none," said Margaret. "Like me."

Lana ignored her. "Are you in Pony Club?" she asked Kim. "What level are you?"

Kim shook her head. "I ... I don't have a horse."

"That's the best part of Pony Club. You don't have to own a horse," said Margaret. "We don't."

"That's not precisely true," said Michelle. "Tim has a pony."

Margaret countered with a grin. "I said 'horse.'"

"Michelle's a D," said Lana. "I'm a D2. It's like grades in school. A is best. If you can write and ride the A test, you're, like, in the Olympics. Then there's B2, B1, B, C2 — like Tim — C1, C, D2, D1 and D. Everyone at Hug a Horse calls Ds babies. Then there's E. That's like pre-Pony Club. Before you write any tests. They're really babies."

"That's me," sighed Margaret.

"Tim's not really a C2," said Michelle.

"He passed the written," said Lana, "and he would have easily passed the ridden if Jelly Bean had stayed sound."

"It was really gross!" said Margaret. "Last summer, the very first day I came here, there was this mega fight. Blood everywhere! Tim's pony got this enormous gash under her back knee!"

"Not her back knee," said Michelle. "Her hock."

Margaret rushed on. "Jelly Bean fights with the other horses all the time. She thinks she's the best."

"She is!" said Lana.

"Well, she hurt a tendon or something, too, and got real lame. Then the vet came out and showed Tim what to do every day until her leg healed, and he said Jelly Bean shouldn't be ridden for at least *two* whole months. So instead of paying a lot of money boarding her at Hug a Horse when he couldn't ride her, Tim put her in a pasture, over at ..." Margaret paused to take a breath.

"At Mrs. MacLean's," said Kim. She surprised herself. She never interrupted anyone. But she liked these girls, and with so much talk about horses, she felt all shivery inside — the words just tumbled out.

"How did you know that?" asked Margaret.

"She's the Cracker kid, remember?" said Michelle. "She lives just up the road."

"Oh, yeah," said Margaret. "I don't know how you can live there. A place like that would give me nightmares."

"There isn't any ghost there," said Michelle. "I just read a book all about Nova Scotia ghosts, and Crackers wasn't in it."

"Enough already," said Lana. "We were talking about Tim's wicked pony."

Margaret nudged Michelle. "She means 'talking about Tim.'" They giggled. Lana didn't notice — or didn't care.

Margaret continued, "Lana hates Jelly Bean because Jelly Bean hates Lana."

"Jelly Bean hates all girls," said Lana. "Anyway, Tim couldn't ride the C2 test because there was no other horse he could borrow that was as good as Jelly Bean."

"Except Star," said Michelle.

They all frowned and nodded.

Suddenly Lana took off at a run. "I get Belle!" she shouted.

Michelle bolted after her. "You did her yesterday. I get her today."

"I called it first. Whoever calls it first, gets it."

"Then I get Belle tomorrow." Michelle puffed, working to keep up with Lana's long legs.

Margaret stayed with Kim. "They fight over which horses to groom," she said. "They all want to be around the biggest horses. Even if I got there first, they'd make me brush the ponies 'cause I'm the newest." She grinned a mischievous grin. "Thing is, I love the ponies the best."

The driveway (it *was* a driveway after all) turned sharply left and ran straight up a long hill with broad green pastures on either side. A large blue sign arched overhead with "HUG A HORSE FARM" in gold letters.

A board fence edged the driveway on both sides. Each section was painted a different color, starting with deep purple, then blue, green, yellow, orange and ending in red at the top of the hill.

"Don't you just love the fence?" said Margaret dreamily. "It's like walking up a rainbow."

Kim nodded. "Where's the pot of gold?" she whispered.

"Are you psychic or something?" Margaret exclaimed. Then she giggled. "No, really. Vanessa, she's the owner, her first horse was named Pot of Gold. He was really amazing — he won tons of trophies and ribbons — but he died three years ago. He's buried in the orchard behind the house."

Then Margaret leaned close and whispered, "Vanessa sometimes sees him grazing under the apple trees."

"She sees him?"

Margaret nodded slowly. "Weird, eh?"

Kim couldn't help wondering if everyone in Meadow Green believed in ghosts.

The top of the driveway forked to a low brick house on the left and a huge chocolate brown barn on the right with a fenced riding ring beside it and an enormous steel barn behind that. Margaret led Kim to the brown barn.

Big double doors were pulled back, filling it with light and cool breezes. The concrete aisle was covered with a heavy rubber mat and was wide enough for a truck. Box stalls ran down each side, shiny brass nameplates on each stall door. It was a perfectly beautiful barn. Too perfect. Where was the chewed wood, the kicked walls, the smell? Where were the horses?

"Ready?" shouted Lana from the far end of the barn.

"Just a sec," said Tim. He slid open the stall door nearest Kim and hooked a rope across the front door opening. "Okay!" he yelled. "Let 'em in."

Lana leaned against the sliding door. It rumbled open and a small herd of horses walked down the aisle.

Kim knew this was no way to bring in horses. What if two went in the same stall? There'd be screaming and injuries. But to her amazement, each horse peeled off into its own box stall, except a roan pony, which trotted all the way to the front, turned around and strolled back down the aisle to the stall closest to the back door. Michelle and Lana walked along, sliding stall doors shut and stroking each eager face that greeted them.

Then Tim led out a big, well-muscled black and white pony. He stood it in the center of the aisle and hooked a rope to each side of its halter. He picked up one of the pony's front feet — large and round ... like the hoof-prints by the brook. The horse flicked its tail — long and black ... like the hairs snagged in the barbed wire.

Kim's smile crashed to the floor along with her mental picture of little white or red or brown Jelly Bean. There was no mystery horse in the river pasture. No surprise for Gramma-Lou. Nothing but her stupid imagination. Stupid, stupid, stupid. It took all her strength not to run out the door, down the driveway and all the way home.

The pony poked out her black nose. By reflex, Kim reached to pat it. A shovel handle intercepted her out-stretched hand.

"Uh-uh," Margaret said, "Patsy will have your hide if she finds out you touched Star without her permission."

"Well, I won't tell," said Tim, putting down the pony's foot.

"Star?" asked Kim.

"Exactly," said Margaret, rolling her eyes. "Leave it to Patsy to pick such a dumb name. Do you see a star? He doesn't have a white hair on his head."

"He? You mean this isn't Jelly Bean?"

"Jelly Bean?" Margaret pointed down the aisle. "She's the crabby pony back there trying to bite Michelle."

A large SUV drove up and dropped off a pretty girl Tim's age. She was dressed in tan breeches and black riding boots. Her salon-streaked hair was precisely arranged in four french braids. She wore makeup.

Tim stroked Star's shoulder. "I was right, Patsy. The shoe is loose," he said to the new girl. "I could tell by the way it clinked on the rocks outside."

Patsy exhaled noisily. "Dad said he's not due to be reshod for two more weeks."

"Well, he's outgrown his shoes. Horses' feet grow faster this time of year. All that moisture and green grass. Why don't you try him barefoot? Vanessa's offered to do the trimming."

"Dad said all that barefoot stuff is hogwash. A horse can't go without shoes."

"What about J.B.? And Vanessa's Canadians? And those warmbloods at Jen V's and —"

Patsy cut him off. "Whatever." She walked past

Margaret and Kim as if they weren't there. She kissed Star on the nose, hanging firmly on to his halter when he tried to pull away.

"Come meet Jelly Bean," Tim said to Kim. He led out the roan pony and put her in cross-ties behind Star.

"See why I couldn't tell you what color she is?"

A smile swept through Kim. She nodded. Jelly Bean was not white or brown or red. She was white *and* brown *and* red — all mixed up together, except for a white patch covering her rump that was speckled with brown and red spots the size of jelly beans. The pony swished her short, sparse tail. Kim sucked in a quick breath — so many colors in that tail, and not a single hair was black.

CHAPTER 9

Hug a Horse

Patsy picked up a curry comb. She looked at Kim. "Do you want to help?"

Kim hesitated. The river pasture and its mysterious resident beckoned.

"I ... I should be going," she mumbled.

"You can get a ride home with me," said Margaret. "My mom will be here in an hour."

Star took a half step forward — sleek and shiny and entirely irresistible. Kim would love to brush him. "Okay," she said, "I'll help."

"Go to the tack room and get Star's saddle and bridle," said Patsy. "The black Kieffer, the black snaffle bridle and the Atherstone girth."

Something about Patsy's manner wasn't quite nice.

"You don't have to," said Margaret, in a tone that said "I wouldn't if I were you."

But Kim didn't mind. She walked past the other girls, each hitching a horse to a set of cross-ties. "This is Belle," said Lana. "Michelle's got Fleur. They're purebred French Canadians."

"Chevaux Canadiens," Michelle corrected. "Sept ans d'immersion et tu ne sais pas encore parler français."

"Don't get her going!" Margaret hollered.

Kim smiled. "Hi, Belle. Hi, Fleur," she said softly to the two red-gold chestnuts with apple rumps and solid builds. They had very pretty heads, straight nosed and big eyed. The standardbreds she was used to usually had long convex heads that bulged between the eyes — hard to call pretty. But Gramma-Lou didn't mind. She'd say, "They can be as ugly as a brush fence as long as they're fast."

The earthy scent of saddle soap and well-oiled leather drew Kim into the tack room. Saddles, perched on red enameled racks, filled the wall to her right. Neatly hung bridles covered the left wall. Plastic brush boxes lined shelves on the back wall. Kim touched the nearest bridle, soft and supple and scented over time by leather soap, oil and horse.

A sudden sadness grabbed her — a homesickness for Mr. Cameron's tack room, with its harnesses hung everywhere, the winners photos and newspaper clippings, the tabby cats sleeping on piles of horse sheets and the comfy chair where the old farm dog curled up on rainy days — and where Kim had spent many an hour coloring or reading or sleeping.

She wiped away a tear and focused on the bridles in front of her. Four of them were black. Three had snaffle bits, one sporting a woven black and white brow band, very flashy — just like Star. Kim hung that bridle over her shoulder and turned to the saddles.

Again, four black ones. But none stood out, said "Pick me." How was she supposed to choose the right saddle? She thought about Patsy's tone of voice, so casual, so not-quite-nice. Kim had that ugly sinking feeling. Patsy knew the saddles looked alike.

Kim ran her fingers over the cantle on the nearest saddle. The name "Kieffer" itched in the back of her brain like a tickle between the shoulder blades you can't reach. Why did it sound familiar? Something to do with the tack shop in Charlottetown. She saw herself there, stroking a dark brown saddle. It was secondhand and still the most expensive in the store. That was it! The lady called it a Kieffer, one of the best brands in the world. She showed Kim the maker's brass plate nailed to the saddle tree up under the skirt.

Kim grinned. She checked the saddles — only one had the Kieffer nameplate. Two girths hung immediately below it. She picked up the Atherstone, curvy with skinnier sections for behind the horse's elbows. She carefully lifted the saddle off its rack. It was halfway heavy. It felt good. She stood there, bridle over her shoulder, saddle over her arm, just like an illustration in the *Manual of Horsemanship*. She could almost feel a helmet on her head and smiled all the way into imaginary tall, stiff boots.

"You need help?" Patsy shouted, in a voice that didn't offer help.

Kim walked quickly up the aisle. "Hi, Fleur," she said clearly before she passed the horse. "Hi, Belle." After a lifetime of summers in Mr. Cameron's barn, she had learned never to approach a horse quietly. Gramma-Lou taught her, "Horses think in only one direction at a time." The mares were paying attention to their grooms. If Kim didn't speak to each one, she might get a surprise kick from a startled horse.

"Hi, Jelly Bean," she said.

Tim looked at the tack she carried. His eyebrows lifted and he smiled broadly.

Michelle, Lana and Margaret watched as Kim approached Patsy. Patsy put down Star's brush and turned to Kim saying, "That's not —" She stopped, mouth open. She took the tack without so much as a thank you.

Margaret dragged Kim out the front door. She grinned from ear to ear. "How did you know what an Antherton girth is?" she hissed.

Kim grinned, too. "An Atherstone," she corrected quietly. "It's in the Pony Club manual."

"Come meet Strawberry," said Margaret. "She's my favorite. I ride her in a lesson every Saturday afternoon. Vanessa lets us do chores in trade for lessons." She led Kim back to Strawberry's stall. "Hi, sweetheart," she said to the elegant bay pony. "I can't groom you today. It's my turn to pick up poo."

Margaret pushed a green plastic wheelbarrow out the back door. Kim followed her out and under a shady lean-to that ran between the two barns. A short, stocky white pony stood in one corner. He had a mane so thick it stuck out in all directions and hid his ears entirely.

"That's Puzzle," said Margaret. "Most of the time he

won't come into the barn. He's allowed to do whatever he wants. He's really old." She groaned. "So much poo! When the flies are bad, all the horses hang out here instead of going over to the pasture or up in the woods. They only come in the barn now when we want to ride or groom them."

Kim nodded — that's why the barn was so clean. The horses didn't live in there. Mr. Cameron kept his broodmares outside all the time, too. But they had fourteen acres to run around in and Mr. Cameron didn't pick up their manure.

Margaret prodded the mounds of manure with a wooden-handled fork — like the fork Kim had always used in Mr. Cameron's barn to sift manure from the sawdust bedding. Margaret wasn't very good with it. She pushed more balls of manure than she picked up.

Tim stepped into the doorway. "Maggie, Lana and Michelle will clean up the riding rings. You sweep the aisle and the tack room when you're done here."

"But that'll take too long. I'll miss seeing you ride!"

"I can help," said Kim.

"Uh-uh," said Tim. "If Vanessa hasn't taught you, you're just supposed to watch."

Kim shrugged and said quietly, "I know how to use an apple picker."

"A what?" Margaret and Tim asked in unison.

"That fork," said Kim. "My grandmother calls it an apple picker."

Margaret giggled. "Maybe that's why Vanessa calls them horse apples."

"Your grandmother has horses?" asked Tim.

"Sort of. She used to train racehorses."

Margaret gasped. "Your grandmother rode racehorses?"

"No," said Kim. "She trained standardbreds ... pacers."

Margaret looked confused.

"Harness horses," Kim said gently. "You don't ride them. You drive them."

"Pacers pace instead of trot," Tim lectured. "Instead of moving the opposite front and back legs together, they move both legs on the same side at the same time. And you sit in a sulky and drive them."

"I knew that," said Margaret.

Tim passed Kim an apple picker. "Well, if you're used to working around racehorses, I guess you'll be safe around Puzzle. Just watch out you don't get licked to death."

Puzzle loved to slobber on any bare skin that came close enough, but Margaret and Kim managed to finish the lean-to without getting drowned. By then everyone else had gone outside. Kim agreed to sweep the tack room while Margaret assaulted the aisle with a broom. The air instantly clouded with choking dust. Kim wished she was bold enough to stop Margaret and show her Gramma-Lou's technique for sweeping without flicking the broom and all the dirt into the air.

When they were done, Kim followed Margaret outside. Heavy clouds boiled up from the south and a stiff breeze hissed loudly through the pines at the far end of the riding ring. They plunked themselves down on a bench next to Lana and Michelle.

"Kim's grandmother trains racehorses," said Margaret. "Not the ones you ride. The ones you drive."

"Your grandmother has horses?" Michelle exclaimed. "Bet you're a really good rider."

Kim flushed. "They weren't for riding."

"Not ever?" asked Lana.

Kim shrugged. No point saying how she used to sneak down to the back pasture and catch Haley, the smallest and quietest of the five broodmares, how she'd tie a rope to her halter and climb aboard. It wasn't any different than sitting on the ponies she and Janis encountered. It wasn't real riding. Real riding was getting the horse to do everything you asked — to go or stop or turn — which Haley definitely didn't do. No, not real riding.

"Too bad," said Michelle.

"I love watching Tim and Patsy ride," said Margaret. "Vanessa says you can learn a lot by watching."

"Where is Vanessa?" asked Kim, a little nervously. She hoped it was okay to be here.

"Friday's grocery day," said Margaret. "Tim's in charge till she gets back."

Tim rode past on Fleur, wind licking eddies of dust off each footfall.

"He's not riding Jelly Bean?" Kim asked.

"Tim's too big for her now," answered Margaret. "Fleur is just four. Tim's helping Vanessa train her."

Kim watched Patsy and Tim ride in large circles, small circles, neat stops and changes of speed — all so smooth. They never pulled or kicked or shouted.

Sometimes Kim didn't see any signals at all when the horses turned or cantered. She sighed. That was real riding. Her whole being yearned to ride like that.

"They're so good," she said.

"The best," said Margaret.

A fat drop of rain thumped Kim on the head. Then another. And another. All of a sudden a wall of water tumbled from the sky. Everyone bolted for the huge steel barn.

Kim found herself in an indoor arena with long translucent panels high overhead that let in the storm-dimmed light.

Tim scooped up two towels and tossed one to Patsy. "Got these from the tack room, earlier. Kind of thought it might rain," he said, and quickly rubbed his saddle dry. "Just managed to squeak in that ride."

"Barely," said Patsy, smiling. She wiped Star's tack. "He went well, didn't he?"

Tim and Patsy led their mounts around the arena to cool them down. Moments later a car drove up. "That's Mom," said Margaret. "Come on, Kim. Run for it." The two girls scurried through the downpour and dove into the back seat.

"This is Kim," Margaret giggled, mopping her face with her sleeve.

"Ah, another horse nut," her mother said, like it was a normal thing.

"Will you be at Hug a Horse tomorrow?" Margaret asked Kim. "My lesson's at three."

Kim shrugged and smiled. She snuggled into the seat and watched the rain-soaked countryside flow past. No going to the river pasture tonight, but she was only slightly disappointed. She'd met four friends, discovered a fabulous horse farm and proved there was a horse in the river pasture. It had been a great day.

And it wasn't over yet! It was only ten after five. Janis would call at six. She'd let Kim talk to Gramma-Lou because Kim would insist like she'd never insisted before. Kim would tell Janis it was very, very, very important — it was about horses. Janis would understand.

CHAPTER 10

Storm

It was a short drive home. Kim could have sworn the bus had traveled much farther. Hug a Horse Farm was an easy bike ride away! Perfect. Absolutely perfect.

Now maybe she could finally get some riding lessons. Gramma-Lou had tried to get her riding lessons in Prince Edward Island. There was a stable nearby but they didn't teach children under twelve. The only other place Gramma-Lou could afford was more than half an hour away by car, and Gramma-Lou never had learned how to drive. Kim had been forced to wait until she was old enough. She was twelve this year. *This* summer was supposed to have been the summer she learned to ride.

Maybe now, with Hug a Horse just up the road and Gramma-Lou here *and* Janis to back her up — maybe now she could take riding lessons. Surely the three of them could keep Colm from saying no.

There were two cars in the driveway when she arrived, Colm's and another, vaguely familiar. Kim waved good-bye to Margaret and rushed up the steps and under the little roof protecting the back door. Colm's visitor must be someone from the university — no one else ever came here. Kim was in no mood to be introduced as the short blond genetics joke. She opened the back door a crack and listened.

Colm sounded annoyed. "Of course I remember you. If you and your husband hadn't interfered, I'd still have a father today."

"Lou would have left Roddy sooner or later."

It was Mrs. MacLean.

"Wrong. Wrong. Wrong. It was *your* fault. Mother would have stayed with him if you hadn't driven us to that goddamn horse farm in PEI."

"Didn't you ever wonder why she called me? An old friend she hadn't seen in a decade? Who lived so far away? Lou was desperate. She had no one else. After all those years in Dartmouth, she didn't have a single friend. Roddy never let her. That's what abusive husbands do. They isolate their wives so no one will find out what's going on."

"Dad was not abusive!" Colm snapped. "He never hit my mother!"

There was a long silence.

Finally Mrs. MacLean said, "I didn't come here to get into this. Let's let sleeping dogs lie."

"Humph."

"I met your daughter the other day. She said Lou was coming to stay here. Surely you know the history of this place."

History? What history? Kim couldn't hear well over the wind and rain. She nudged the door open a little more. She could see Mrs. MacLean at the kitchen table, her back to the door. Colm sat across from her, shuffling through the pile of mail.

He huffed. "Don't tell me you believe those stupid ghost stories, too."

"But Lou's father ... your grandfather ..." A gust of wind shoved the back door wide open.

"Oh, hello," said Mrs. MacLean.

Kim had no choice but to go in.

Colm ignored her. "My grandfather sold the farm and moved the family to Halifax. End of story. Everything else is hogwash."

Mrs. MacLean nodded her head slowly up and down. The tightness in her shoulders said she was holding something back. Kim could see she wasn't used to that.

"I'll be going now," said Mrs. MacLean. "Be sure to call me when Lou gets here."

As she rose and unhooked her cane from the back of the chair, the baseball on the curio shelf caught her attention. She sucked in a breath.

"Is that the ball? Your father's baseball?"

Colm's dark mood broke like sunlight through heavy cloud. He took three quick steps to the shelf. "You know about this?"

"My, yes," she said, gazing sadly at him as if he were suddenly a badly injured puppy. "Doesn't it upset you to keep it around?"

The clouds closed in. With renewed annoyance, Colm launched into his story. "This baseball was signed by the great Babe Ruth himself. The Bambino signed it for my father when Dad was eight years old. See? It says 'To Roddy, from Babe Ruth.' My grandfather was a guide on the St. Mary's River. He took the Babe on a fishing trip, and Ruth caught eight salmon as long as my father was tall. He was so grateful he signed this ball, just for Dad. It was my father's prize possession, and he gave it to me the day you took me and Mom away. It's worth at least two thousand dollars now."

"I see," said Mrs. MacLean. "I imagine you've been telling that story for so long you actually believe it."

"I beg your pardon?" Colm said. "This is an actual Babe Ruth baseball."

"I know it is," said Mrs. MacLean. "Lou told me about Roddy and his baseball in her letters."

She turned her back to him and shuffled to the door. "She told me everything," she muttered on her way out.

Colm sat down at the table and snatched up an envelope. He ripped out the contents and growled a teeth-clenched curse. Colm hated bills. He only opened them to avoid something worse.

"You're late," he snapped. "Where were you?"

"I met some friends," Kim answered.

"What's that god-awful stink? Is that horse? Where have you been?"

"There's ... there's this nice farm up the road."

Colm slammed down the bill. "How many times have I told you to stay the hell away from horses? Horses will ruin your life. Just how stupid are you?"

Kim folded inward like a balloon with a slow leak. "I was only looking."

"You should have been home when Janis called."

"But she wasn't supposed to call till six," Kim gasped.

"She had to call while Mother was asleep," he barked, as if Kim should know that fact.

"But I needed to talk to Gramma-Lou."

Colm struck the table with his fist. "You *can't* talk to Gramma-Lou."

"But I *need* to talk to her."

He bolted to his feet, chair crashing backward, his scar glaring white on red. "Haven't you been paying attention?" he roared. "Your grandmother has Alzheimer's!"

"When she gets better ..."

"For christ's sake, use your brain. She's not going to get better."

Kim's lower lip trembled violently. "But they have new medicines ..."

"She's not going to get better."

"I *really* need to talk to her about something."

"Well, you can't. She doesn't remember *anything!*"

"She remembers me."

"*You?* She can't remember *me.* Why the hell should she remember *you?*"

He might as well have stabbed Kim with a knife. She just stood there, slashed to pieces by his words. Feet, hands, voice, brain — all disconnected.

Colm kicked the fallen chair out of his way, stomped into the den and switched on the television.

Somewhere between the blare of MTV and Tweety Bird, Kim found her voice. "Gramma-Lou would *never* forget me!" she screamed.

She fled outside. The storm still dragged its rippled gray belly over the valley. The rain had stopped, and the damp air hung motionless.

"Gramma-Lou would never forget me," she sobbed. "Never!"

She ran toward the river. Rain-heavy blackberry canes arched into the path, snagging her sleeves and pant legs, bombarding her with water. By the time Kim reached the riverbank, she was soaked to her underwear.

She ran on, past the fish trap, daring anyone to be there — to try to stop her. No one was. No one did. She didn't stop running until she collapsed under the spruce trees in the middle of the river pasture.

She curled up on the thick layer of needles, soft and dry beneath the dense, drooping boughs. Her sobs mingled with the sounds of the brook — burbling, bubbling, steadily soothing, soothing.

Clearer thoughts welled up. They were always doing research, finding new drugs. Gramma-Lou could get better. Colm exaggerated. He exaggerated everything — especially when he was mad.

Gramma-Lou would never forget her.

All old people forgot some things. The last time Kim visited, two summers ago, Gramma-Lou called her Lynn a lot. That wasn't forgetting — it was remembering. Mrs. MacLean had said Kim looked a lot like Gramma-Lou's sister Lynn when Lynn was twelve. And there was the time Gramma-Lou put the milk in the cupboard and the cereal in the fridge. When they discovered the mistake the next morning, they laughed so hard they fell out of their chairs.

Okay, Gramma-Lou forgot to turn off the stove a few times and left the kettle to whistle itself dry, but Kim caught those things. And when they were walking in the dunes and Gramma-Lou insisted home was in the opposite direction, Kim reminded her that the dunes had just been totally redesigned by the worst winter in thirty years. Anyone might have had trouble finding the path home.

An exhausted calm sank through Kim. She sat up and rubbed her eyes. The spruce shadows seemed unusually dark. Had she fallen asleep? She looked at her watch. No, only six o'clock. She wandered into the field. The roiling black-gray sky looked so solid that Kim felt, if she were tall enough, she could run her fingertips along its bubbled contours. It was beautiful and frightening at the same time, like flames in a bonfire.

The field and wood huddled hushed in the gloom. Even the birds had gone to bed early. So quiet, save for the song of the brook and, in the distance, the wind growing steadily louder, pushing over the long hills toward the river pasture, rustling and hissing strangely, like angels in taffeta skirts. The gloom deepened as the sound grew nearer, harder.

"That's not wind," she gasped. "That's rain! Buckets of rain!"

She debated for a fraction of a second whether or not to risk the shelter of the leaning barn. The hiss grew to a roar — it was the barn or drown. Kim pounded for the old building as fast as her legs could carry her.

Heavy, stinging drops slapped her heels as she dashed into the dark structure. The outside world turned liquid, all shapes and colors washed away, all sounds lost to the din of drumming on the steel roof high overhead. Then a deep moan, rising quickly to a roar, filled the world with wind. The barn shuddered and the rain slanted in through the gaps in the wall, chasing Kim down the center aisle and up and over the tumbled bales of hay.

To her surprise, she found the center aisle didn't end in a pile of lumber. It was the wall of a large horse stall. In the dim light, she admired the barn's posts, full, round trees as thick as a hug. Hand-hewn beams skillfully slotted into them made the barn much more solid than it appeared from outside. Kim stepped into the stall. The exposed earth floor was smooth and dry. A suggestion of wood shavings lingered along the margins. She hauled in a hay bale, pried off one string and folded the bale open. She pulled apart all the flakes and sagged down into the sweet, herblike scent of a past summer.

Outside, the storm roared on. Kim marveled sleepily at how a building with so many holes in one wall could be so cozy. Somewhere a loose board fluttered in a gust — like the sound of a horse blowing dust from its nostrils. The dampness pulled a musty, almost horsey smell from the walls and floor. Kim fell asleep smiling.

When she awoke, soft light reached into the barn, tickling the far corners of the stall. She would have lain there longer, savoring the stillness, if it hadn't been for the smell. She couldn't breathe. Not because of the thick odor, but because of the overwhelming realization that she hadn't been the only one to seek refuge from the storm. There, immediately in front of the stall, lay a fresh pile of manure.

Kim scrambled to her feet, but the barn's corners held

no secrets. She walked quickly outside. A thick mist hugged the river and spilled over into the pasture. Standing knee deep in a gilded cloud carpet, as if floating like an angel, was the horse. He lifted his head and shook it vigorously, spraying a bright halo against the golden light. Kim gasped. It was like a scene from a wonderful dream — except for the horse.

He had a forelock so full of burdocks it stood up between his ears in a lump the size of a grapefruit. His tail was a club of burdocks that whooshed and thumped his rump when he swatted at the small blackflies that clustered over the weeping sores on his hocks. Those raw patches of skin were the only parts on the horse's whole lower half that weren't encrusted in manure. A frizzy, faded winter coat still clung in ragged patches on the upper half of the poor beast, and a frayed halter hung on his head, its original color masked in filth.

Kim was speechless. Not even a curse could express her disgust and horror. Even the very worst of the backyard ponies didn't come within miles of looking this bad. She wanted to grab the person who let this happen and scream at them at the top of her lungs.

A tiny breeze swirled the mist around her, drawing with it the horse's damp stench. Kim nearly choked.

"You smell like a dead cow," she gagged.

She walked slowly toward him. "Hi there, horse," she said soothingly. "Where were you yesterday? Were you hiding in the barn? Can't blame you for hiding. If I were you I wouldn't want to be found, especially by the creep who let you get like this. But you don't have to be afraid of me. I won't hurt you."

The horse watched her carefully.

"Where'd you come from? Did you run away? You're a smart horse if you did. How come I never saw any ads for a lost horse? Maybe whoever lost you doesn't want you back. That's no stretch. Then again, maybe somebody already rescued you and put you in here. No, then you still wouldn't be such a disgusting mess. Did you find this place on your own? Did you jump the fence? You must have jumped the fence. You're certainly tall enough to do that."

The closer Kim got, the bigger the horse seemed. His withers, at the top of his shoulder, were well above her head. She held out her hand.

"You were smart to stay in this pasture with all this grass to fatten you up. Jelly Bean stayed here last year when she was injured. She got all better here. This place makes a good horse rehab. You can stay here as long as you want. I won't tell anyone."

His left ear flicked at her words. He stretched out his neck and blew a hot, moist breath on her hand. Kim grinned and reached to touch his neck. The horse stepped lazily just out of reach. Kim tried to touch him again, and again he stepped away.

"I won't hurt you," she promised.

Three steps forward. Her fingertips brushed his shoulder. The horse tucked in his chin and lifted away at a trot. Kim followed. When he stopped, she reached out, and away he went again, cutting through the mist, which swirled and evaporated in his wake. Over and over, around the pasture the horse led Kim or Kim pushed the horse.

She wasn't sure which. She lost track of how many circuits they made. The mist had swirled to nothingness. Her legs felt like overcooked noodles. She stumbled and dropped into the wet grass, tears leaking down.

"How can I help if you won't let me touch you?"

The horse lowered his head and began to graze, still ten steps out of reach. Numb with disappointment, Kim rose and headed for the river.

She felt more than heard him behind her. She turned. He stood at arm's length, watching her calmly. Kim backed up a step. He followed. She gingerly took hold of his halter, half expecting him to toss his head and rip her arm from her shoulder. He just blinked at a fly.

She stroked a tiny patch of summer coat on his neck. He tipped his head and leaned into her touch. She could feel his eager energy through her fingertips. She sighed with relief. "You feel a lot better than you look! You're happy here, aren't you? And you're so itchy!" She scratched vigorously until he leaned so far over she was afraid he'd fall on her. Her fingers came away black and greasy.

"Man, do you need a bath! I'm an expert at bathing horses. 'Cept I'm used to a hose and warm water, and no horse I ever washed was as dirty as you are. But I can do it. You'll see.

"I'll come back tomorrow morning with some buckets." She started a mental list. "And sponges, and soap, lots of soap, and brushes, and a rope, and apples — I'm not chasing you tomorrow." Kim kissed the warm velvet just behind his nostril. "See you in the morning, you sneaky horse, you ghost horse you."

Kim planned her Saturday as she hurried home. "First I'll wash the ghost." She smiled. It was a good name for him. "That could take all morning. I can still go to Hug a Horse in the afternoon. I can ask Tim or one of the girls if they know about a lost horse, but I'll have to be careful. Ghost needs to stay lost for now. He's safe in the river pasture. He has food and water and shelter. He has me to groom him and to love him ... and maybe even ride him."

~

Dark kitchen, loud TV, snoring — nothing had changed and everything had changed. There's a horse in the river pasture!

Kim climbed into some dry clothes, then scraped together dinner and ate without tasting. *A real live horse!* She was sure she'd explode if she didn't tell Gramma-Lou. She snuck the phone up to her room and dialed PEI.

Janis answered. "Kim, dear, I'm glad you called. Things are moving more slowly than expected. I didn't find someone to take the cottage till today."

Kim got a sudden cramp in her stomach. "Take the cottage?" she echoed.

"Didn't Colm tell you?"

"He got mad."

There was a long pause. "He's just worried about your grandmother coming to stay. Listen, I need you to switch your bedroom with the one we set up for Gramma-Lou."

"The room over the studio? But Colm said Gramma-Lou needed her privacy."

"Gramma-Lou needs to be where we can keep an eye on her, not at the opposite end of the house. She needs your room. We'll be there first thing Sunday. You'll have to move your stuff tomorrow."

"Tomorrow? But ... I can't."

"Kimberly, never say can't." There was a loud noise in the background. "Oh god, got to run."

"But I need to talk to —" Click.

Kim stared at the phone until the dial tone startled her. She climbed into bed. Tears suddenly overwhelmed her. Someone bought the cottage. She was never going to see Gramma-Lou's periwinkle blue cottage again. Never. She had practically grown up in that cottage — the only constant in a lifetime of change.

But Gramma-Lou would be here soon, she consoled herself. Here in this very house. She set her alarm for six. She'd move her room early so she still had time for all her other plans. Colm was not going to be happy about the move. She needed to be finished before he got up.

~

The rain thundered down on the barn, washing away the red paint, like blood, puddles of bright, fresh blood. A voice, the girl's voice, screamed at the thunder, at the rain, at the red running down to the river.

CHAPTER 11

Wash Day

Kim felt like she hadn't slept at all. The same dream jolted her awake three times. She opened her eyes as sunlight tipped the western hills. Two thoughts jumped up simultaneously, blotting out the night fear: There's a horse in the river pasture. One more day till Gramma-Lou. Her exhaustion vanished.

She leaped out of bed and looked around her room. She liked this room. Was this the room Gramma Lou had slept in when she was little? Kim wished she didn't have to move.

Her room, her parents' room and three other bedrooms at this end of the house all opened onto the hallway at the top of the kitchen stairs. The smallest held Janis's sewing machine, tiny TV and the bed she used to escape the worst of Colm's snoring. The other two were filled past the windowsills with Colm's junk. It'd take a backhoe to empty them.

She tiptoed downstairs, through the living room and up the narrow stairs to the bedroom at the far end of the house. Sunlight spilled through two large windows. Muted green walls spanned the house's width. The room was huge. And quiet — far from Colm's snoring. Far from everything. The only furniture was a dingy little dresser and an old bed that Janis had found at a yard sale. They would do until Gramma-Lou's furniture was shipped from PEI. Then Kim could get her own stuff back.

Gramma-Lou would have loved this big bright space, but Kim had to admit the stairs were very steep and the bathroom was half a house away. Janis was right. If Gramma-Lou was still not feeling well, this bedroom wasn't a good idea.

Then Kim realized that if this was her room, she could slip downstairs early every morning and go outside through the painting studio below. No one would hear. No one would know. She could visit Ghost and be back before they even thought of her.

She knew where the studio key was hidden. Janis kept the studio locked "to keep Smudge out." Kim knew it was to keep Colm's criticism out. Janis had never tried to hide her work before, but then she never had her own room to paint in before. Kim silently promised Janis she wouldn't look at the paintings. She knew how important privacy was.

Scooting back to her old bedroom, Kim began pulling things out of drawers and off walls. It had taken her days to decorate, arranging and rearranging posters, stuffed toys and her bits of furniture until it was perfect. It took only minutes to pile everything onto the bed and begin hauling it down the stairs, through the house and up the back stairs, one armload at a time. When she finally lined up her eleven model horses and Gramma-Lou's photo on top of the little dresser, she didn't think she could climb one more step.

She staggered down to the kitchen and gulped a bowl of cornflakes. Then she grabbed two plastic buckets Colm used for watering his plants, shoved one bucket inside the other and packed in a sponge, dish soap, scrub brush, rope, ointment and four apples. She plastered sunscreen and fly dope on all exposed skin and slipped quietly out the back door.

The morning stood in glorious opposition to last night's storm. The sun pressed green perfume from every leaf and blade of grass. The air hung so thick and still that the newly freshened river sounded an arm's length away. A chickadee landed on the empty bird feeder and scolded, "Chicka-dee-dee-dee."

"Go find some bugs to eat," Kim scolded back and danced through the field, swinging the buckets in exuberant pirouettes.

She marched boldly along the narrowed riverbank, unconcerned about the fish trap ahead. It was Saturday. She'd never seen or heard anyone coming or going on Saturdays.

A sudden pounding noise slowed her happy feet. She walked carefully forward until the trap came into sight. There they were — two men standing waist deep in the river, hammering on a piece of fish fence collapsed by last night's high water.

Kim's heart banged against the buckets clutched to her chest. What was she going to do? She couldn't risk sneaking past Mrs. MacLean's house. If she got caught again, Mrs. MacLean would know something was up. She had to go past the fishermen, past two total strangers. And here in Nova Scotia that was terrifying.

In PEI it had been just her and Gramma-Lou and horse people she had known all her life. In big cities, walking past strangers on the street was uncomfortable but at least they ignored you. Here in Nova Scotia, no matter who you were or where you went, strangers spoke to you. "Cold enough for you?" "Nice day, eh?" "Good day for a duck." And the most terrifying part — they expected a reply.

Today the two men were busy fighting with the current, so maybe, just maybe ... Head down, staying close to the alders, Kim focused on each foot, forcing it forward. She almost collided with the puke green pickup truck. She looked up. The taller man, hip waders dripping, stood near the tailgate. He nodded and smiled, white teeth brilliant against dark chocolate skin. Kim melded to the rocks. He opened his mouth to speak when his partner yelped and fell head first into the river. The man dashed to his aid, choking with laughter.

Kim silently screamed to her feet, MOVE! Miraculously, they obeyed, and with each step fear leaked away.

She did it! She walked right past them! She grinned in triumph. When it came to Ghost, she'd walk past the devil himself.

She climbed up the bank. Dew silvered the grasses of the river pasture. Ghost's morning wanderings brushed darker green paths through the dampness. Kim could see where he'd walked around the field twice, almost on the same path but not quite — as if two horses had strolled side by side.

Kim approached him casually, indirectly, hoping he wouldn't take off like yesterday. He didn't. He took one look at the buckets, wuffled softly through his nostrils and marched straight up to her.

"You want treats? Well you've come to the right place, mister." She dug out an apple. Ghost chomped it in two and waggled his muzzle up and down, slobbering apple-foamy saliva up her arm.

"They're a little sour, aren't they?"

She quietly slipped her rope through the halter ring under his chin, led him to the brook and tied him to a thick branch. Then she pulled at a lump of ancient manure caked to his hair. It stuck like cement. Ghost flapped his tail and stomped one hind foot.

"Sorry," said Kim. "I'll try soaking it off."

She filled the buckets from the brook and sponged and sponged and sponged. The crust took forever to soften into a foul, brown sludge. Kim used a stick to scrape it away one slimy layer at time. All the while, Ghost stood quietly, eyes half closed, tail thumping at flies.

It took twenty buckets of water to free the horse's lower half from the filth. She discovered his mane and tail were black, but his belly was a very dark brown, and tan tinged the hair between his back legs, just above his black muzzle and on his lower eyelid.

"You're not a black horse after all. You're black-bay," Kim told him.

She poured half a bottle of soap into a full bucket of water. Her neighbor in Vancouver did this to bathe his greasy-haired Newfoundland dog. Using the second bucket as a stool, she sponged the soapy water over Ghost. She tried scrubbing with the brush, but it clogged with hair on every stroke, so she went at him with her hands. Brown hairy suds squished between her fingers. As her fingertips reached his itchy hide, Ghost leaned over so far he kept knocking her off her bucket.

Kim persisted, massaging every inch, being extra gentle around the sores on his hocks and the big scar she uncovered on his hip. She rinsed and sponged and scrubbed and rinsed and sponged and scrubbed again. At last, his sour stench yielded to lemony freshness.

Ghost began fidgeting and pawing the ground. "Yeah, I need a break, too." Kim untied him. He stepped hesitantly away, then abruptly snaked his neck and exploded upward in three grand leaps, punching his hind feet skyward. Just as abruptly, he dropped his head to graze.

Kim lay spread-eagled in the sun, squinting at Ghost's lean body. From a distance the scar on his hip looked too neat to be accidental, too symmetrical. The more she stared at it, the more she knew it wasn't an accident — it was a brand. The letter H maybe, with the sides curved in. Or two horse heads on arched necks facing away from each other. Or both. She thought they only branded Western horses, but Ghost was no cow pony. He looked more like an extra-large racehorse.

Her batteries recharged, Kim ate two apples and lured Ghost back with the last. She looped her rope into a makeshift halter, removed the horse's filthy one and scoured it to a faded red. Then she put it back on, tied Ghost in the shade and set to work on his tail. "The secret is to take the hair from the burdocks, not the burdocks from the hair," the Newfoundland-dog owner had said. Both seemed impossible. She picked and picked, teasing wisps of hair from the solid mass. Burr hooks chewed her fingertips, but she ground her teeth and kept at it. Slowly tufts became locks and locks became a tail.

The mane eventually hung neatly as well, though a bit sparse in spots. The forelock proved the biggest challenge with its fine, slightly frizzy hair. Ghost held his ears back, concerned but polite.

Finally all that was needed was ointment gently spread on his hocks. Then Kim kissed him on the nose and untied him, stepping well out of kicking range. Ghost trotted away, tossing his head and flipping knots back into his mane. Kim swelled with pride. She imagined Gramma-Lou's surprised face when Kim told her what a mess the horse had been.

Her watch said three o'clock. The bath had taken years longer than planned. She hoped she still had time to catch the end of Margaret's lesson and ask a few careful questions about lost horses. She gathered her supplies and hurried toward home.

At the bend in the river, Kim peeked through the alders. The man who had fallen earlier was standing on the long pole that levered the trap out of the water. The other man shoveled salt into a barrel. As she approached, he rolled the barrel up to the truck. He wasn't looking her way. She put her head down and kept a steady pace past the truck.

He spoke to her back. "Beautiful day," he said. "That black horse yours?"

Kim stopped dead. Her brain offered only one response. She nodded.

"Figured," said the man, and smiled. "My son owns a horse, too. Maybe you know him?"

Kim couldn't breathe. She stared at him, jaw slack.

The man shrugged and went back to shoveling. "City kid," he said to his partner.

Kim turned and speedwalked home. The black horse wasn't hers. She had lied. But what difference did it make if a perfect stranger thought she owned a horse?

Gramma-Lou always said lies come back to haunt you.

~

As usual, Colm had gone to the office after Saturday morning cartoons. Just in case he returned before she did, she wrote two identical notes — "home for supper" — and taped one to the fridge and one to the TV screen. She wasn't going to give him an excuse to be mad at her today.

The bike ride to Hug a Horse took eight minutes. Eight uphill minutes. Kim's thighs burned as she pushed her bike up the driveway past the rainbow fence.

The girls were in the outside ring, but it looked like the riding lesson was over. They stood beside their mounts as a slightly plump lady in green breeches and brown leather boots was demonstrating something to them, shifting her weight back and forth on each leg, hands out as if holding reins.

Kim sat on a bench and doodled with her toe in the damp sand — a right-facing horse head, a left-facing horse head.

"Hi, Shrimp," said Tim, plunking himself down beside her.

Kim spooked sideways.

"Easy, girl, easy."

"You riding next?" Kim asked, eager to watch his skill again.

"Nah. Just gonna lunge J.B. I'm too tall to ride her now."

Kim nodded. "Lana told me. So why don't you buy a horse?"

"My parents think horses take me away from soccer too much as it is. Besides, I couldn't afford one unless I sold J.B."

"So why don't you sell her?"

"Can't. No one else can ride her."

"She bucks people off?" asked Kim. She suddenly wondered if Ghost would do that.

"Just the opposite," Tim groaned. "She balks. Won't move an inch. Except backward. It'd be funny if she wasn't such an evil little thing. She's also not real fond of girls."

Lana opened the gate at the far end of the ring and led Belle into the barn.

"Got to go," said Tim. As he stood, he glanced at the sand by Kim's feet. He picked up a stick and drew the curved lines longer and crossed the H. "That's more like it," he said, and walked toward the barn.

Kim stared at the sand. That *was* more like it. Exactly like it.

CHAPTER 12

The Disease

Kim's mind reeled. Tim knew exactly what Ghost's brand looked like. Had he seen Ghost?

A bright voice startled her. "That brand looks familiar."

Kim looked up into sparkling hazel eyes.

"Hi, I'm Vanessa," said the lady in the green breeches. "And you are?"

"This is Kim, the girl I told you about," said Margaret, dragging over a reluctant Strawberry.

Vanessa nodded toward the sand. "The Hanoverian brand. You dream big."

"I saw one on the Internet," said Margaret. "They wanted fifty-five grand for it!"

"Some of them are pretty pricey," said Vanessa. "They're excellent jumpers and dressage horses. They're starting to become more common in Nova Scotia, but I've only seen a few, myself."

She shooed Margaret toward the barn. "That pony needs to be groomed before she's turned out."

Margaret called over her shoulder, "Kim, you coming or what?"

Kim picked up her bike. She looked at the drawing in the sand. Was Ghost a Hanoverian? Maybe Tim hadn't seen Ghost. Maybe he had seen one of the Hanoverians Vanessa saw. Half of Kim desperately needed to find out more. The other half desperately needed to get on her bike and pedal back to the river pasture as fast as she could. And stay there forever.

She pictured Ghost grazing happily, his deep, dark eyes, the gloss of his freshly washed coat, the tan velvet behind his nostrils, his burdock-free tail swishing, swishing over his ointment-covered hocks, the round, raw holes of missing hide ... the feeding flies. She let out a long, shuddering breath, dragged her sneaker across the drawing and pushed her bike toward the big barn.

The aisle was filled with horses and swarming with un-tacking, brushing, hugging riders, all chatting and laughing, serious and silly and definitely noisy. All but Tim, walking calmly from the tack room, a saddle and bridle in his arms.

Jelly Bean stood nearest the door. As Kim approached, the pony lifted her tail and plopped a steaming pile on the rubber mat.

"Thanks for the present," said Tim. "Kim, will you get that?"

Kim grabbed an apple picker to pick up the manure before Jelly Bean stepped in it. She sensed Vanessa watching her. Was this a test? If she didn't push the fork, bounce, bounce, bounce it just right, and scoop ...

Vanessa walked over. Kim tipped the manure into a

wheelbarrow. "So, let me see," said Vanessa. "You have, hmmm, eleven model horses in your bedroom."

Kim flashed Tim a look that begged "How does she know that?"

Tim answered in a creaky old-woman voice, "Everyone knows everyone's secrets around here."

"Looks like I got lucky with the number." Vanessa chuckled. "But owning model horses is a symptom of the Disease, and Tim told me you've got it really bad."

Kim flinched. Disease?

The girls paused mid-purpose and watched her intently. Their sudden silence pushed her backward against Jelly Bean's shoulder. The pony strained the limit of the cross-ties and blew hot breaths down Kim's collar.

Vanessa continued, counting off a finger at a time. "Other common symptoms are: reading every horse book you can get your hands on; plastering your walls with horse pictures; doodling horses all over your scribblers; bucking, rearing and whinnying; tying reins to the handle bars of your bicycle; building snow horses instead of snowmen; answering the question 'What do you want for Christmas?' with 'A horse, of course' so often that now you just say 'You know' ..." Vanessa stopped to catch her breath, then pursed her lips and muttered, "Let's see. That's eight. I know there's more."

"Bookmarking every 'Horse for sale' site on the Internet," Lana offered.

"When you see a horse, your palms *itch*!" Michelle said "itch" with such energy the left corner of Kim's mouth twitched upward.

"And your favorite perfume is the smell of horse," said Margaret, planting her nose in Strawberry's mane and inhaling deeply.

"That's eleven," said Vanessa. "And don't forget hiding horsey clothes in the back of your closet so your mother won't wash them."

"Or hiding something else!" shouted Lana.

The girls burst out laughing. Michelle waved a dandy brush at Margaret. "Was Margaret's mom ever mad when she found a hat full of manure under Margaret's bed!"

Margaret melted into a pile of giggles.

Vanessa groaned, then added, "I forgot favorite numbers."

"Mine's five, of course," said Lana, "because there are five letters in 'horse' ... second is four, for 'pony' or 'mare.'"

"Mon numéro à moi, c'est le six — pour 'cheval'!" said Michelle, kissing Fleur.

"And, and," said Margaret, still giggling contagiously, "mine's eight for 'stallion.'"

"Well, Kim," asked Vanessa, "how many symptoms do you have?"

Kim knew all those symptoms — all things she'd been criticized for or embarrassed by, or had hidden. Jelly Bean lipped her sleeve. Kim fiddled absentmindedly with the pony's halter.

Vanessa leaned back, looking slightly disappointed. "*Any* symptoms?"

Kim nodded.

"How many?" Vanessa prodded, playfully.

"All of them," Kim whispered.

"Aha!" exclaimed Vanessa. "You were right, Tim. She's one of us!" She beamed triumphantly, her smile as irresistible as balloons and puppies and three-layer chocolate cake.

Kim's whole body smiled back. "One of us" bounced around inside her, knocking over stacks of shyness.

To her own amazement, she heard herself ask, "So where'd you see those Hanoverians?"

"At a dressage show in the Valley," answered Vanessa.

In Nova Scotia, the "Valley" meant the Annapolis Valley. Two weeks ago, Colm had taken them there to see the Apple Blossom Festival, but there weren't any apple blossoms left. Spring had sprung weeks early. He had grumped all the way home, making the four-hour drive feel like a week.

Ghost couldn't have been one of the horses Vanessa saw.

"I heard some European guy bought a farm in Cape Breton," said Tim, tightening Jelly Bean's girth. "Imported a bunch of Hanoverians from Germany."

"That's right," said Vanessa. "He was going to breed and sell horses for the dressage market. He certainly couldn't have done his homework. Cape Breton is as close to the dressage scene as Earth is to Mars!"

"Does he live near Sydney?" asked Margaret. "I saw two Hanoverians at a show in Sydney last year."

"You wouldn't know a Hanoverian if it stepped on you," Lana called from Belle's stall.

"The lady sitting behind me said they were Hanoverians," Margaret retorted. "And they both had that brand thing."

"They could have been quarter horses," said Tim. "I've seen lots of brands on quarter horses — circles, letters, symbols, all sorts of different things."

"Yeah," said Michelle. "They were probably quarter horses. What did they look like?"

"They were really big and really tall. And their brands looked just like the one Kim drew," Margaret answered.

Trying not to sound too interested, Kim scratched Jelly Bean's freckled forehead and asked, "What color were they?" Jelly Bean leaned happily into her touch.

Margaret didn't answer. She looked at Kim funny. Vanessa was looking at her funny, too.

"Darn, forgot my lunge whip," said Tim. He threw Vanessa a sideways glance and passed Jelly Bean's bridle to Kim. "Will you put this on? I'll be right back."

Kim took the bridle, glad for the change of subject. Had she asked too many questions? Did they suspect she was hiding something? She stood on Jelly Bean's left side and lifted the bridle over her face. Jelly Bean opened her mouth and fairly dove for the bit, practically putting the bridle on herself. "Good girl," said Kim.

Maybe she could talk to Margaret later, when Tim and Vanessa weren't around. Maybe one of the horses Margaret had seen was Ghost. But Cape Breton was a big island, two hours by highway from Sydney to the causeway, and another half hour to Meadow Green. No, Ghost couldn't have traveled from Cape Breton on his own.

Kim looked up. Margaret was staring, now openmouthed. Tim had stopped halfway down the aisle and was also staring. In fact, everyone was staring.

CHAPTER 13

Want to Buy a Pony?

Kim's cheeks flushed red hot.

"She let you put the bridle on," Margaret whispered, as if a louder voice would break some magic spell.

"Amazing!" Michelle crowed.

Tim walked up and slapped Jelly Bean lovingly on the neck. "You evil little beast! And here I thought you hated all girls!"

Everyone started talking at once.

"Do you remember the time she shoved that Gillis kid ..."

"... and those yellow teeth coming right at me!"

"She stood there for an hour in the pouring rain ..."

"I'm lucky to have my thumb ..."

"... with both back feet!"

Jelly Bean ignored them all, calmly lipping hot horse kisses on Kim's arm. Kim rubbed her under the jaw. Jelly Bean responded by reaching her nose skyward and poking out her upper lip in itchy ecstasy.

The verbal chaos folded into laughter.

"You've got the magic touch," said Tim. "Want to buy a pony?"

"You could keep her at your place," said Lana.

"And we'd come and visit all the time," Margaret chimed in.

Kim shook her head. "My father hates horses."

"Yeah, my dad thinks they stink," said Michelle. "Hey, you could keep her at Mrs. MacLean's where she stayed last year. That's real close, and we'd still come and visit."

Lana gave Michelle a sharp jab with her elbow. "Not there," she hissed.

Tim got a strange look on his face. "That barn has ..."

Lana's eyes flashed. "Oh, we might as well say it." She threw her hands out dramatically. "Ghost. That barn has a ghost."

All the blood drained from Kim's face. They knew!

Margaret jumped to her aid. "It's not that barn. It's Crackers' ... I mean ... Oh, there's no such thing as ghosts. That story isn't true. Right, Michelle?"

"I didn't say there weren't any ghosts. Just not *that* ghost."

"Everyone in Antigonish County didn't just make it up," Lana protested. "There really was a guy who went crazy and shot all his cows and horses — and himself."

"He actually shot his horses?" Margaret moaned.

Vanessa interrupted. "I'm sure it's just exaggeration. Stories can get pretty colorful over time."

Kim blinked. They weren't talking about her Ghost. They were talking about Crackers' ghost. She was too relieved to be upset that they believed that stupid story. "Colm said it isn't true. My great-grandfather sold his farm and moved the family to Halifax," she said. "Simple as that."

"See!" Margaret exclaimed.

"Who's Colm?" asked Lana.

"My father."

"You call your father by his first name? Doesn't he get mad?"

"I think it's cool," said Margaret.

Not to be thrown off course, Michelle said to Lana, "There, Crackers didn't kill himself, so there can't be a ghost."

"Not Crackers' ghost," Lana said impatiently. "The ghost is a horse. Tim saw it in Mrs. MacLean's barn last year."

"Lana," Tim growled.

"Oh, for Pete's sake, what's the big secret?" said Lana.

"A horse ghost?" Margaret said with awe. "You saw a horse ghost?"

Tim grunted. "Pretty much."

"Pretty much what? What did you see?" Michelle demanded.

"Weird noises, shadows, hoofprints," said Tim reluctantly. "Stuff like that."

"You're making it up," said Margaret nervously.

Tim shrugged. "Believe what you want. I'm just glad J.B.'s not staying there anymore."

He marched back to the tack room and returned with a long coiled line, a whip and a black velvet-covered helmet.

"What size are your feet?" he asked Kim.

"Huh?" Kim was still puzzling over what he had said. Did Tim really believe in a ghost or was he putting them on? And why would he do that?

"What size are your feet?" Tim repeated.

"Um, seven."

He turned to the other girls. "Who's got size seven boots?"

Margaret pried off her rubber riding boots. "Try these."

"Is it all right with you?" Tim asked Vanessa.

"I'm as curious as you are," she replied.

Tim passed Kim the helmet and Margaret's boots. "Let's find out just how much Jelly Bean likes you. You can ride while I lunge her."

Kim's heart rate doubled. Did he actually offer her a ride? But she couldn't get on Jelly Bean in front of everyone. She would make a fool of herself.

"I can't ride," she whispered.

"But your grandmother's horses? You must have learned —"

"You don't ride them," said Margaret. "You sit in the cart."

"I've only ridden bareback," Kim apologized.

"A person's got to have good balance to stay on bareback," said Tim. "You'll be fine."

"I don't know," said Kim. Then she remembered. "I thought you said she balks."

"Right. So what do you have to lose?"

Kim stroked Jelly Bean's speckled neck. The pony exuded calm comfort. Kim took a deep breath. If Jelly

Bean didn't move, it wouldn't be her fault. She snapped on the helmet and hauled on the boots, hot and sweaty but a perfect fit. She followed Tim and Jelly Bean to the outside ring. Everyone tagged along.

Tim tightened Jelly Bean's girth and shortened the stirrups. "Mount up," he said.

Kim went to Jelly Bean's left side. She nervously fiddled with the stirrup, not sure which way to place her foot.

"I'll show you," said Tim. "Your foot goes in this way." He twisted the stirrup to the front, placed his left foot in, put his left hand over the pony's withers and his right hand on the back of the saddle. His right leg bounced once, then swung up and over Jelly Bean.

"And to dismount, drop both stirrups first, put your left hand on the front of the saddle and swing over like this." He swung his right leg over the pony's back to meet the left. "Now put your right hand on the back of the saddle." He paused a moment, resting his weight on his stomach, then slipped to the ground. "Like that," he said, then he demonstrated one more time.

Kim's hands shook as she held the stirrup. She stretched up her leg and placed her foot in. She tried to imitate what Tim had done and mounted without his grace but smoothly enough not to upset Jelly Bean.

Settling down in the saddle was like coming home. This was where she was born to be.

"How does that feel?" Tim asked.

Kim grinned. She knew by his smile that he already knew the answer.

She placed her toes in the stirrups. Tim showed her how to hold the reins. Then he hooked one end of the lunge line to Jelly Bean's bridle and backed up. "Give her a little bump with your legs to make her walk."

Kim did as she was told. The pony didn't move.

"She wasn't paying attention. Try again," Tim ordered.

With the second bump, Jelly Bean flicked an ear and stepped forward into a relaxed, energetic walk. A collective gasp rose from the rail. Kim laughed out loud in surprise.

They walked four circles around Tim while he explained how to halt. "Lean back a bit and stretch your heels down and back a little while squeezing her barrel gently with your legs. Don't pull on the reins! Just hold your hands firm so they don't go forward when her head does."

So much to think about at once! Back, legs, hands. On Haley or the ponies, Kim just hauled back on the rope to stop. Sometimes it worked. Sometimes they went faster. Kim tried to do a halt like Tim instructed, but Jelly Bean kept walking.

"Relax," said Tim. "It's hard for everyone at first. You just forgot about your heels. Try again."

Kim tried again. Back, heels, legs, hands. Jelly Bean's ears swiveled around and she hesitated briefly.

"Almost," said Tim, "but you're holding your breath. And next time, don't stop giving the aids, the signals, until she comes to a complete stop. Now lean, stretch, squeeze and breathe — all at once."

Kim tried a third time. She had an urge to haul back on the reins, but she wanted to do it right. She wanted to learn real riding.

She tried again. Nothing. Finally, on the fifth try, Jelly Bean halted.

"That's it!" Tim cheered. Everyone on the rail applauded loudly. "Okay," Tim ordered, "forward and try again."

Kim nudged Jelly Bean forward to a walk and stopped again. They walked and stopped, walked and stopped. Kim beamed. It was easy!

"Do you want to try to trot?" asked Tim.

Kim nodded eagerly.

"Same signal as for walk, only a little more energetic," Tim said.

Kim took a deep breath. The pony's ears turned to her. It only took two tries to get a trot. Kim giggled at Jelly Bean's springy action, not the spine-jarring bumpity-bump she was familiar with.

"Try a rising trot," said Tim. "Let the pony lift you out of the saddle when the outside shoulder goes forward, stay up one step and come down. I'll tell you when. Up, down, up, down, up, down. That's it! You're a natural, Kim."

Total happiness bubbled through Kim. Riding had never felt so good.

They circled a few times. Then Tim had Kim halt. He changed the lunge line on the bridle and they rode circles at a walk and trot in the other direction.

Finally Tim said, "Time's up. Dad will be here soon. You did great, Kim."

Kim sighed and halted Jelly Bean. She couldn't stop grinning. The instant she dismounted, Margaret squealed, "You have to buy her!"

"She likes you!" Michelle cheered.

"Pretty neat," said Lana. "I wouldn't have believed it if I hadn't seen it with my own eyes."

"You have to buy her!" Margaret repeated.

"Okay, okay," Vanessa shushed. "How about we start with Kim taking lessons on Jelly Bean? I'll give you a lesson registration form. I need your parents to sign it."

A pickup truck drove in the driveway.

"Freaking fish guts, that's Dad," Tim growled. His gaze bounced back and forth between the lunge line and Jelly Bean's saddle. "He'll have my hide if I'm late for soccer."

"It's all right," said Vanessa. "Kim and I will put Jelly Bean away."

Tim smiled a thank-you and bolted to meet his father. Kim didn't smile back. The truck was green — puke green. And as it turned by the barn, its smell swirled around her, suffocating her joy with the stench of gaspereau.

CHAPTER 14

Slug

Kim coasted all the way home, her thoughts spinning faster than the wheels of her bicycle. How could she have been so stupid? She should never have nodded to that fisherman. He was Tim's father!

She had told Tim's father the black horse was hers. Now he would tell Tim. And Tim would come to the river pasture and see Ghost and know he's not Kim's and call the animal shelter ... or find Ghost's owner.

Everything was ruined! They'd take Ghost away and she and Gramma-Lou wouldn't have a horse to visit. All her plans were wrecked.

When she got home, she found her note to Colm still stuck to the refrigerator. So was the one on the television.

"That's odd."

Smudge agreed with a hungry yowl.

"Are you in *again*?"

She scooped tuna-stinky cat food into his dish. Her stomach forced her to grab some food for herself —

peanut butter on toast, quick and easy. She sat at the table to eat. It was bare. Not even an unopened envelope.

"Not good," she muttered.

She went up to her new bedroom. She hid Vanessa's registration form in her sock drawer. Then she stuffed her bridle into her knapsack and headed for the river pasture. She was going to get a ride on Ghost before Tim went and ruined everything. She deserved at least one ride after all her hard work washing the horse.

The river pasture seemed empty. No longer afraid of the leaning barn, Kim ventured inside and found Ghost in the stall, half-asleep. His droopy ears pricked at her arrival.

"How 'bout a ride?"

Kim looped the reins over Ghost's neck and took off his halter. Ghost took the bit calmly, and Kim adjusted the bridle the way Gramma-Lou taught her — two fingers under the noseband, four fingers in the throat-lash, and one wrinkle in each corner of his mouth.

"I'm going to need a ladder to get on you."

She led him out to the gate and pushed him sideways against it. He moved over willingly, but when she climbed the gate, he swung to face her, his back out of reach. She tried again and again, taking deep breaths to release her growing frustration. If he knew how desperately she wanted to be on his back he might never stand still.

Finally, for a few moments, Ghost froze with his head up and nickered toward the brook. Kim clambered on, wriggling into position just behind his bony withers. She looked at the brook but couldn't see what had interested him. Ghost shifted his balance, his long back muscles flexing under her. The ground looked a lot farther away than Kim expected.

"Wow, are you tall!"

Ghost's ears looked at her. She bumped him gently with her legs. He stepped into a crisp walk along the fence. Kim tugged gently on the right rein. Ghost bent his neck and continued straight ahead.

"Don't you know how to turn?"

She pulled his head around. He turned and marched across the field.

Kim grinned and sighed into the swaying movement. Here she was, wandering around a field on a huge horse, just like Gramma-Lou had on Domino. For a long time she let Ghost walk where he pleased. The low sunlight warmed her face, matching the warmth beneath her. A white-throated sparrow whistled joyfully from the tip of an alder branch, ignoring their passing as if they were just one beast.

After a long while, Kim couldn't help wondering what Ghost's trot would feel like. She nudged Ghost to go faster. He instantly lifted into a huge, bouncy trot, tossing Kim skyward with every beat, nearly thumping her supper back up her throat. She tried to do a rising trot, but without stirrups to push against, she had to pinch her knees tighter in order to lift herself up.

Ghost trotted faster.

"Whoa, Ghost," she ordered.

She pulled back on the reins. Ghost leaned against her pull, hind legs thrusting powerfully, front legs stretching farther forward. The brook rushed at them. Kim grabbed a fistful of mane. Ghost jumped the water and landed at a canter. Kim landed a little too far to the left.

Bounce. She slipped farther down his shoulder. Bounce. The mane ripped from her fingers. Bounce. She crashed to the ground and slid six body lengths through the grass and into a small mountain of crumbly, fly-infested manure.

A reflex glance ensured her she was still alone. No one saw her fall. Ghost sauntered over, turned and added another pile nearby.

"So this is where you hide it. No wonder I never found any manure when I first looked for you. You're one of those picky poopers."

The grass was deeper here, hiding the manure well. There was probably another toilet in one of those spots of taller grass alongside the barn. She remembered that one of Mr. Cameron's geldings fastidiously pooped in the same place all the time. When someone accidentally left the wheelbarrow in his spot, he just filled it with manure, saving them the need to shovel.

Kim shook brown bits from her T-shirt. It was pretty much composted, no smell left. She grabbed Ghost's reins as they trailed by and stood up slowly, feeling muscles she didn't know she owned.

"I bet I could have stayed on if I had stirrups," she said, and led Ghost back to the stall. She traded bridle for halter and hung the bridle outside the box stall on a nail that seemed to have been put there for that purpose. She applied more ointment to Ghost's hocks and wondered again how a purebred Hanoverian ever got in such a state.

A raspy creak interrupted her thoughts. Ghost tensed. Somebody was opening the gate. That would be Tim, of course. His father was sure to have mentioned the black horse and the blond girl with the buckets. Tim was bound to check it out the minute his soccer game was over.

A shadow drifted across the wall. A male voice hissed, "Hey, Wheeler. Are you in there?"

A thump hit the aisle. And a second thump. Two apples rolled into the patch of sun just inside the gaping doorway. Ghost hurried toward them. Kim followed close behind. As she stepped past him, her heart turned to lead.

The voice did not belong to Tim. It was Slug's.

Terror bolted her backward into the deepest darkness of the barn. She crouched behind a broken wooden door, panting. Slug hadn't seen her! Just as she had stepped into view, he had turned away, distracted by something near the brook.

Through a crack, she could see from the bright doorway all the way back to the box stall. She almost sobbed aloud. Her knapsack leaned against the stall wall — in plain sight.

Another thump. Kim watched a third apple roll into the barn. Queasy with fear, she fought to think. Even if Slug walked into the barn right now, it would take a minute for his eyes to adjust. She didn't need a minute. Creeping forward, she reached for the bag, lifted it silently and crept backward. She collapsed in a sweating heap in the shadows.

The light dimmed slightly. Slug stood in the barn entrance, bulging kit bag in one hand.

"Hi, Wheeler. Getting nice and fat for me?"

He tossed another apple deeper into the barn. Ghost followed. Slug dropped the bag and pulled out a huge coil of rope. He tied one end to the exposed post on one side of the door opening and strung it at waist height to the other side, then back again at chest height, creating a rope barrier.

"I'll get you this time," he said.

He rolled the fifth apple all the way into the box stall. Ghost didn't move. Slug took a shorter rope and a bullwhip from his kit bag and walked toward the horse.

"Into the stall."

Ghost stiffened, head up, ears back. He took a half step to the left.

"No you don't!" Slug jumped left.

Ghost deked right and two steps forward. Slug countered right. Ghost forged left, hooves skidding. Slug jumped into his path, loosing the coils of his whip.

"Back up, you black demon!"

Slug raised his arm and brought it down hard. The whip swished through the air and smacked the hay softly. Slug roared curses and tried to snap the whip again. A loud whoosh. A splat.

Ghost danced tightly in place. Then he collected his weight onto his haunches and plunged ahead at full gallop. Slug gaped in horror. Ghost smashed him aside, ducked his head and lifted at the same time, flying between the top rope and the beam above. He vanished down the hill at top speed. A moment later, even the sound of his hoofbeats disappeared.

Slug groaned. Then a string of curse words poured out with growing volume and venom. He kicked and kicked the hay bales, grunting and cursing, cursing and grunting. At last he turned and walked out of the barn.

Kim thought she heard the gate creak, but she wasn't sure. She didn't dare move. What seemed like hours passed. When she finally looked at her watch, only fifteen minutes had ticked away.

She waited another five minutes before shouldering her knapsack and easing herself along the aisle to within view of the gate. No Slug. The whip and rope lay at her feet. She grabbed the whip and ran for the river faster than she had ever run in her life. She ducked through the fence and kept running until she reached the blackberry path and her own backyard. There her knees dissolved. She sobbed against the hard earth. She sobbed for Ghost, for her anger, for her fear. She choked on tears until the well was dry, nothing left but a blank, empty hole.

Ages later she found herself numbly staring at the whip in her hand. Suddenly she leaped to her feet. "How dare he hit Ghost!" she raged. "How dare he!"

She lifted the whip and drove the lash down and back. The tip exploded with an ear-splitting crack.

The back door opened.

"Is that you, Kim?" Janis called.

"You're home!"

Kim crammed the whip into her knapsack and ran into the house.

"Where's Gramma-Lou?"

Colm hissed, "Be quiet! She's finally asleep. I'm going to bed, too." He dragged his feet up the stairs as if they were made of wood.

"I thought you weren't coming till tomorrow," Kim said to Janis.

Janis sighed. Weariness had smudged dark shadows under her eyes. "Lou demanded to be taken home today."

Kim frowned. "But you *left* her home."

"No, not that one. This one. This is her home now ... again."

Janis spread her arms, inviting a hug. "I missed you. How's my little Kimbit?"

"I missed you, too." Kim fell into the hug.

Janis wrinkled up her nose and pushed Kim away. "Whew! Where have you been? You're filthy."

Kim grinned. "I found this horse —" She stopped. Janis never could keep a secret. "I found this horse farm just up the road! And I got to ride this amazing pony and on a real English saddle!"

"You did that? By yourself? That's wonderful! I'm so proud of you."

"You and Gramma-Lou have to come and see it."

"That may not be so easy." Janis took a deep breath that grew into a forever yawn. "I'm exhausted. Why don't we talk about this in the morning? Go wash up — and make sure you're quiet. Gramma-Lou is a light sleeper."

Kim climbed into the shower. How was she ever going to sleep? Thoughts of Gramma-Lou and Ghost and Slug spun like a Tilt-A-Whirl out of control, flinging her emotions in every direction at once.

She could hear her father's full-throttle snore before she turned off the water. If Gramma-Lou could sleep through that, she could sleep through anything. But just to make sure, Kim tiptoed all the way through the house to her room. Then she got an idea. She picked up the glass with the ivy cuttings, tiptoed back to her grandmother's room and silently placed the glass on the bedside table. She hovered a moment, staring at the profile of her best friend.

"I love you, Gramma-Lou," she whispered.

Tomorrow she would tell Gramma-Lou about Ghost. He wasn't her surprise anymore. He was Slug's horse. But Gramma-Lou would know how to make sure Slug never hurt Ghost again.

Kim curled up into a tight ball under the blankets, pleading with her heart to slow down. "Deep breaths, deep sleep," Gramma-Lou used to say. Deep breaths, deep sleep.

❧

She was riding again. But the horse beneath her was golden and it galloped blindly through a sea of rain, away from the horror, away from the man's voice shouting for them to stop — shouting her name and her name was Lou.

Chapter 15

Gramma-Lou

"I can't find Mama."

Kim opened her eyes, barely half awake. Moonlight flooded the floor. Gramma-Lou stood in the doorway.

"I can't find Mama," Gramma-Lou repeated.

"She's in the room across the hall from your bedroom," Kim mumbled.

"Someone moved the blanket closet."

"The what closet?"

"I'm cold. Can I sleep with you?"

"Sure."

Kim scrunched to one side of the three-quarter bed. Gramma-Lou curled next to her, shivering noticeably.

"I missed you so much," whispered Kim. She snuggled up to her grandmother. "This is just like when I was little and I used to climb into bed with you."

"Yes," said Gramma-Lou. "'Night, Lynn."

Kim giggled. "I said when *I* was little, not when *you* were little."

Gramma-Lou giggled, too.

~

Kim awoke alone. The sun was well up, and the house very quiet. She tiptoed to her grandmother's room. The bed was empty, the blankets slumped on the floor. The sheets were pulled halfway off, like someone had started to strip the bed and gave up. The air smelled of urine. Kim backed out quickly and closed the door.

The toilet flushed. Kim tapped on the bathroom door. "Gramma-Lou?" she whispered.

Janis stepped out of the bathroom. She looked like she hadn't slept in weeks.

"Oh, I thought you were Gramma-Lou," said Kim.

"She's probably still asleep," said Janis groggily.

"She's not in her room. She ..." Kim blushed. "She had an accident in bed."

"Not again. Where is she now?"

Kim shrugged. "She's not downstairs."

Janis snapped wide awake. She leaned into each of the other three bedrooms. No Gramma-Lou. "Kim, check downstairs again."

"I just came through the den and the kitchen. She isn't there. And your studio's locked."

"Then be quick and check outside. She's probably just out sitting in the sun. She likes the sun."

Janis got dressed and caught up with Kim in the front yard. There was no sign of Gramma-Lou.

"Okay, okay," Janis told herself. "Big things, little things."

She took a deep breath, let it out partway, then shouted, "Oh, hell! This is big. I've got to wake your father."

"I'll look in the barn," Kim offered.

"I don't think she'd go in there, but you better check anyway."

Kim went to the barn. Its front door hadn't been opened. Colm's white-bagged winter tires were stacked against the door, waiting since April to be put inside. She trotted around back and hollered, "Gramma-Lou, are you in here?" Not a sound stirred the cobwebs.

Kim returned to the house. She heard Colm through the ceiling. "What do you mean, gone?"

"Where would she go?" Janis demanded.

"How should I know?"

"She's your mother, for christ's sake! She must have told you about her childhood here. A favorite place or something."

"Not a goddamn word."

"She must have. Think, damn it!"

"She doesn't even know where she is."

"What are you talking about? She knows this house. She grew up here." Janis's voice stretched like a rubber band about to snap.

"Can't you keep track of her for one night? How the hell are we going to do this for the whole summer?"

"We?" Janis gasped.

Silence reigned as Kim climbed the stairs. "She's not in the barn," she said quietly. "Maybe she went to visit Mrs. MacLean."

"Of course," said Janis. "Of course. Good thinking, Kimbit. Colm, check the rest of the property and then go up the road. I'll go down the road and check with Mrs. MacLean. Kim, stay here in case Lou comes back."

Colm stomped down to the kitchen. An instant later he began to roar. "*Arrrrrrr!*" Like the wail of a siren, rage and panic twisted together, louder and higher and higher and louder, "*ARRRRRRRRRR!*" to the ragged limits of his vocal cords.

Janis flew downstairs — a moth to the searing flame.

This could be bad, thought Kim, really bad. Or it could be just another emotional outburst by the master of exaggerated emotional outbursts. She walked halfway down the staircase. Colm was standing in the middle of the kitchen, his right arm raised, finger pointing to the glass case on the shelf where his baseball was supposed to be.

"She took my baseball!" he bellowed. "She took my baseball!"

"First things first," Janis said bluntly. "I'm going to Mrs. MacLean's."

"We have to find it!"

"We have to find your *mother!*" Janis slammed the door behind her.

"Kim, you search this house." Colm waved his hand like an orchestra conductor without rhythm. "Everywhere!" he bellowed. "I'll look outside."

"What about Gramma-Lou?"

"You find that ball!"

And he was gone, sucking the anger out the back

door with him. Kim walked slowly to her room and got dressed. What was the big deal? So Gramma-Lou moved his stupid baseball. The useless thing just sat there. What did it matter that it was worth thousands of dollars if Colm never intended to sell it? And what was the big deal about Gramma-Lou going for a walk? She went for a walk every morning. Colm and Janis freaked about everything.

Kim rammed her sock drawer shut. The photo of Gramma-Lou and Domino toppled on its face. She stood it up. The happy pair stared at her from the sloping green field with the line of spruce trees and the river beyond. Kim suddenly realized she knew exactly where this picture had been taken. The field was identical today, except the trees were taller and broader.

"That's where you went!"

She ran outside and stopped dead. What about Slug? Would he be around at seven-thirty on a Sunday morning? No way. She had seen him half-asleep every morning all year — every morning, that is, when he had actually dragged himself onto the bus.

~

Kim found Gramma-Lou in the river pasture sitting under the copse of spruce. She wore a sweatshirt and sweatpants, both inside out as usual — seams bothered her sensitive skin. Same old Gramma-Lou. Kim smiled.

Nearby, Ghost caught the morning rays, ears lazily paying attention.

"Hi, Gramma-Lou! I see you found the horse." She sat beside her grandmother. "I was hoping to surprise you. I was hoping you and I could come over here every day and visit him, you know, groom him and stuff, like we always do. But I found out yesterday that he belongs to this creep who tries to beat him. Gramma-Lou, we have to help him."

Gramma-Lou didn't seem to react. She looked at Kim. "Did you come to visit Domino, too?"

Kim wanted to say, "I didn't call him Domino," but the words bunched into a huge lump in her throat. The most wonderful person in the whole world was just sitting there, looking at her, her smile a reflex of uncertainty, and her eyes — there was something big missing from her eyes, something huge, like summer without sunshine.

Kim could barely breathe. Fear clawed at her heart.

Gramma-Lou turned away, humming. With a fingertip she traced the curve of a huge hoofprint in the moss. Then she rubbed one hand over the other, as if trying to rub away the liver spots on her translucent skin. "He waited for me," she said wistfully.

Kim forced words past the horrific tightness in her throat. "Who waited?"

Gramma-Lou's brow crinkled. She looked at Kim. "It's your turn to make breakfast," she said. A glint of familiar sparkle lit her eyes. "What are we having?"

Kim bit her lower lip to keep it from trembling. Relief twisted through her. She centered on that sparkle.

"Your favorite." Her voice shook badly. "Scrambled eggs and molasses."

"Who ever thought of putting those things together?"

Kim forced her cheeks to smile. "You did," she whispered.

The walk home went slowly. Gramma-Lou kept stopping to collect pebbles. She'd compare the newest pick to the one in her hand, decide and toss one away. It was an old ritual they had performed on the beaches of PEI. They returned home with the one most special stone to remember the day by, to add to the memory stones overflowing the little baskets on the dining room table.

Just as they reached the blackberry path, Gramma-Lou turned around and headed back down along the river. Kim called after her, "Gramma-Lou, you're going the wrong way."

The old woman just kept walking. Kim caught up with her.

"Gramma-Lou." No reply.

"LOU!" Kim barked.

The old eyes focused. "Hi, Lynn. Are you coming to see Domino, too?"

"No," Kim moaned in frustration. "It's me, Kim." Gramma-Lou looked confused and worried. Kim sighed and said, "We just saw him."

Sudden panic shot from her grandmother's eyes. She clenched Kim's forearms with astonishing strength.

"Don't tell Papa where he is." Her breathing was quick and shallow. Tears flowed down her face.

Kim gulped. "I won't. I won't."

The darkness slowly faded, replaced by an unsettling blankness. Gramma-Lou wiped her sleeve across her face. Kim forced back tears. She took her grandmother's hand, and they walked home in silence.

As they passed the bird feeder, a saucy squirrel chirped at their nearness from atop the feeder roof. Gramma-Lou smiled and pointed. "Furry bird."

Kim glanced at the empty feeder, only it wasn't empty anymore. The baseball was tucked behind the Plexiglas.

"Colm's baseball!" said Kim. Gramma-Lou grabbed her arm.

"No," she keened. "Gone."

"But it's Colm's."

"Nooo," Gramma-Lou repeated, a heartbreak of sorrow pouring out of the word.

"But he's so angry," Kim argued halfheartedly. She couldn't imagine why her grandmother had hidden the ball, but her look was enough to leave it hidden. Hand in hand, Kim and Gramma-Lou went into the house.

Colm leaned against the stove, beating a bowl of eggs with vicious energy. He nearly spilled the yellow froth when Kim and her grandmother came in the door.

"Mother, you're back," he said. To Kim he asked, "Did you find my baseball?"

"I found Gramma-Lou."

Colm put on that soft, little boy look he used when he wanted something from Janis. "Mother," he asked, "where did you put my baseball?"

"Baseball?"

"Yes!" said Colm excitedly. "You took my baseball out

of the case —" He pointed to the shelf "— and you put it ... where?"

"He took it," she said.

"No, Mother." His jaw tightened, beard jutting out. "You took it. Where did you put it?"

Gramma-Lou clasped her hands to her chest. "Colm was so sad," she moaned.

Colm choked back a growl. "I'm Colm! Where did you put my baseball?"

His mother smiled — a bright, empty smile. She shook her head and said firmly, "I don't want to play with you." She sat at the table.

Colm ground his teeth on a curse.

"I'll call Janis," Kim muttered. As she picked up the phone, Janis and Mrs. MacLean came in the back door.

"Lou! Oh, thank god," said Janis, sinking into the seat next to her mother-in-law.

Mrs. MacLean sat across from Gramma-Lou. "Hello, Lou. I'm Erika. Remember me?"

"Did you come to visit Mama?"

Erika shook her head and patted her old friend's hand.

"You'll stay for breakfast," said Janis.

"She lost the goddamn baseball." Colm pouted. Janis nailed him with her eyes, then rose and took out the frying pan, banging it loudly on the burner.

The hard lump had returned to Kim's throat. Breakfast seemed pointless. She quietly climbed the stairs and sat out of sight on the landing, curled up cross-legged, tears soaking her shirt.

Butter sizzled. Eggs hissed. A spatula stirred and

stirred, then scraped and clinked as eggs were served to waiting plates.

"Kim, breakfast is ready," called Janis.

Kim stayed put.

"A foof. A grabber," said Gramma-Lou.

"Colm, pass her a fork," said Janis.

"I forgot," said Gramma-Lou.

"It's okay," said Janis. "That happens to everyone when they get older."

Colm coughed nervously. The utensil drawer rattled.

"Yes, a whatsawhosis," said Gramma-Lou and giggled. Erika laughed with her.

"Ricky?" asked Gramma-Lou.

"Yes!" answered Erika. "It's Ricky. Hello, old friend."

Her friend chuckled. "Old, yes, old." She mumbled the last through a bite of breakfast. "Needs molasses."

A chair scraped. The fridge door sucked open and closed.

"Ricky is your nickname?" Janis asked.

"Yes," said Erika. "Everyone around here has a nickname."

"For example," Janis prodded, clearly desperate for casual conversation.

"Don't get me started," said Erika. But she was. She told them name after name and almost as many stories of how each name came to be. There was Step Stool and Knee-high, who never grew very tall, and Handsome Hughie, who was *not* attractive, and Johnny Fat, who was as thin as a pin. They all laughed about Joe Ninety, who drove too fast and his brother Sam Forty-five, who lived his life at half-speed.

And Kumpy, Pookey, Ugga and Poss, who got their names as toddlers and kept them till they died.

"And there's our neighbor Holler."

"What neighbor?" asked Janis.

"Just past my place, in the foundation with the roof. His boy, Slugger — loves baseball, I think — would be on the same bus as Kim."

"Doesn't anyone have a real name?" Janis exclaimed. "So is the father H-o-l-l-e-r or H-a-u-l-e-r?"

"Well, both actually. He hauls animals, mostly cattle, but it's his voice he's notorious for. When he's angry, which is all too often, you can hear him bellow all the way to Guysborough. Some days I have to close my windows."

"That must be the idiot who lost the load of cows," said Colm.

"Load of cows?" asked Janis.

"Yeah, last month I was having lunch with the dean at the steak house on the highway when this cattle truck pulled over. The driver got out and started hollering at this black horse in with the cows. The horse went ballistic and kicked the tailgate off, and the whole lot unloaded themselves right onto the Trans-Canada."

Janis gasped. "Was anyone hurt?"

"No, but it took the better part of an hour to round them up. The ass kept screaming at them."

A fork dragged across a plate, and Colm mumbled through a mouthful, "Don't think he ever did catch the horse."

Kim's jaw dropped. So that's where Ghost came from! Colm had known all along! She dried her face on her shirt and bumped down three steps to see into the kitchen. The conversation had paused. She waited for Colm to say something more, like which way was Holler coming from, which way the horse went. But Colm just shoveled in more eggs.

Gramma-Lou ticked her nails rapidly on her empty plate. Her blank smile sagged badly.

"I wonder what happened to the horse?" asked Janis, trying to restart the conversation.

Gramma-Lou's smile melted completely. "He wouldn't stop screaming," she moaned. She leaned across the table and grabbed Erika's arm. "He wouldn't stop!"

"It's okay, Lou," Erika soothed in her most musical tone. "It's okay now."

But it wasn't okay. Gramma-Lou's moaning couldn't be quieted.

"I'll take her to her room," said Janis. She led her up past Kim, talking on about the weather, the new vest she just made, the color of the walls — everything and anything — desperately searching for the magic words to calm her mother-in-law.

Kim sat helpless, struggling not to cry again. She wanted to go to Gramma-Lou and hug her and say, "Hi, Gramma-Lou. It's me, Kim," and everything would be okay. She didn't and it wasn't.

Erika blinked back her own tears. She turned to Colm. "You should have known better than to bring her home after what happened here."

Colm rolled his eyes. "You're not going to go on about that again. That story's just not true."

"Denying the truth doesn't change it," she said, then left.

The screen door banged shut. Gramma-Lou's moaning ceased soon afterward. The upstairs went quiet. Water gurgled down the pipes from the bathroom. Colm got up and started rummaging around the house, opening and lifting and moving and cursing.

Kim went to her room. Mrs. MacLean was right. Colm shouldn't have brought Gramma-Lou here. Kim should have gone to PEI like always. Gramma-Lou had been fine in PEI. Everything had been fine in PEI. She wasn't supposed to be here. It wasn't supposed to be like this. Kim collapsed on the bed in a heap of sobs.

∽

It was past noon when she awoke. The fragrance of grilled cheese filtered up from below, along with a light girlish giggle from Gramma-Lou. She sounded like herself. Kim wished she could run down and see her, but what if Gramma-Lou called her Lynn again? It wasn't funny anymore. It was scary.

Kim frowned and hugged her knees tightly over her confused heart. She fixed her thoughts on Ghost, remembering what Colm had said about Holler and his runaway horse. They had to be the same horse. The Pomquet River ran behind the steak house. Ghost must have wandered along the river all the way to Mrs. MacLean's. Slug found him there and shut the gate. But why didn't Holler come for the horse? Why wasn't Ghost returned to his owner?

Because Slug never told his father he found the horse! That was it. But what did Slug want with Ghost? And what if he went back to the river pasture today? He'd discover someone had taken his whip. He knew Kim lived nearby. What if he came looking for it? What if he came looking for *her*?

The rest of the afternoon passed with unbearable slowness. Kim hid in her room, jumping at every sound. She thought about returning the whip. She ached to see Ghost, to hug him, to make sure he was safe. But he wouldn't be safe if Slug got the whip back! And Kim wouldn't be safe if she ran into Slug!

Maybe if she talked it over with Janis. Maybe Janis could help. No. Stealing was stealing. Janis would make her give the whip back. Then Janis would try to talk to Slug and his father. But Janis couldn't handle it when Colm raised his voice. She would be no match for a man called Holler.

At supper, Kim tried to tell Gramma-Lou about her year at school. Her grandmother responded a little. She called Kim by name twice and Lynn three times. She told Janis she liked her. She said to watch out for him, he couldn't be trusted. Janis didn't ask who — she said Gramma-Lou got less coherent when she was tired. A good night's sleep would help.

Gramma-Lou never spoke to Colm.

And Colm was too grumpy to speak to anyone. After supper he rifled through the whole house three or four times, hunting for what wasn't there.

His mother kept looking out the window and insisting

it was getting late and she should be going. There were horses to be fed. Janis made Kim try to convince her that Mr. Cameron had fed the horses already. Gramma-Lou's insistence finally faded to an empty smile.

The rest of the evening was just as empty. Kim went to bed early. Her weary heart dragged her into sleep.

~

The world of her dream was nothing but rain, pounding, screaming rain. She was drowning in the water. She was drowning in the fear.

CHAPTER 16

Behind the Dumpsters

Kim gasped awake, desperately trying to push down the heavy fear. She longed to be little again, to crawl into bed with Gramma-Lou, safe from nightmares. But she wasn't little anymore. Now nightmares could happen when she was awake.

She was afraid to be with Gramma-Lou. It was like she wasn't her grandmother anymore, and at the same time she was.

And she was afraid for Ghost. Who was going to help him? Not Gramma-Lou. Not Janis, and certainly not Colm. Who could save him from Slug?

Tim.

Tim knew Slug and Tim knew horses. Tim would help.

The house was dead quiet. Her alarm clock read 7:39. Six minutes to the bus! She'd forgotten to set the alarm! Kim dove for her clothes and her knapsack and tore out of the house praying to the god of better days that Tim would be on the bus.

She could hear the beast in the distance banging over potholes. Kim sprinted up the driveway. The bus rattled into sight. Kim's legs ached. She pushed harder. Brakes squealed. The bus door opened. One-one thousand. Two-one thousand. Three-one thousand. Four — Kim hit the bottom step without breaking stride. Five-one-thousand. Six — up and in. She grabbed the post, spun left and launched herself straight at Tim's seat, hitting the vinyl with a smack as the bus jolted forward.

Tim asked casually, "You ever think of going out for the track team?"

No time to be shy. "Slug," Kim gasped. "Slug ... Slug's found the horse."

"What horse?"

"The one in the river pasture."

Tim looked at her like she had just grown a third eyeball. He glanced around the bus, then whispered, "The ghost?"

Kim shook her head violently. "No. Didn't your father tell you?"

"Dad? Tell me what?"

"About the horse in the river pasture."

Tim raised one eyebrow. "A real horse?"

Kim's mind reeled. He didn't know — until now. But Ghost needed help. "Yes," she hissed. "A real horse! And if Slug catches him, he's going to beat him! You have to help!"

Tim shook his head. "What would Slug want with a horse? He hates horses."

Kim ripped open her knapsack. "He was going to beat

him." She dumped the bull whip into Tim's lap. "I stole it."

Tim gasped. "That's Holler's cattle whip!" He stuffed it back into Kim's bag. The bus slowed to its next stop. Slug's.

Kim hunkered down in the seat.

Tim whispered, "We can't talk about this now. Meet me at recess behind the dumpsters."

The dumpsters! Kim didn't go near the dumpsters. The two cavernous blue bins stood behind the mudroom wall in the school's blind spot. There were no windows there, no teachers' eyes. That's where substances were smoked, test answers traded, plots hatched, fights finished.

Slug climbed aboard with unusual energy. His eyes flashed darkly toward Kim's seat. He loomed over her like a vulture and dropped a plastic bag in Tim's lap.

"Recess," he snarled. "Behind the dumpsters."

His brother shoved him from behind. "Gonna sit with the sissies?" Slug punched him in the arm and stomped to the back of the bus.

Tim opened the plastic bag. A well-oiled bridle lay inside. Kim sucked in a breath. Her bridle. She'd forgotten all about it.

Tim didn't say a word, just studied his knees all the way to school. As the bus pulled to a stop, he ordered, "Stay put!"

Slug walked backward down the aisle, glaring at Tim all the way. Then he was gone, yelling after a gang at the mudroom door.

"The dumpsters. *Now*," Tim ordered.

Kim followed, dodging through the current of bodies drawn by the bell.

Tim stopped in the space between the two rusty blue behemoths.

"Talk."

Kim took a deep breath and began. "Last week I saw this black horse from the bus — only Mrs. MacLean said the black horse died twenty years ago. But then I found a real horse and he was filthy. So I caught him and I washed him. Then Slug came and he had all this rope and he called the horse Wheeler and he said 'this time' he'd catch him, like he'd been there before, and I think he's been trying to catch him for a while because my father says a horse escaped from Holler's truck last month. Slug was really mad. He was going to beat him. I saw him try to use the whip. Then Ghost, I mean Wheeler, nearly ran Slug down and got away and Slug got even madder. He was so mad he forgot the whip. After he left ..." She gulped for air. "I took it."

Tim said nothing for what seemed like forever. Finally he asked, "The horse escaped from Holler's truck?"

"Colm saw a truck loaded with cows and one horse. They ran onto the Trans-Canada. Slug's father caught them all except the horse. Colm said it was black. Wheeler is black — almost."

Tim pulled the bridle out of the bag. "And this?" He asked.

"It's mine. I ... I forgot it in the box stall."

He handed it to her. "Give me the whip."

He stuffed the whip in the plastic bag and hung it from one corner of a dumpster. He started to walk away.

"Aren't you going to help Wheeler?"

"Nope. And I doubt his name is Wheeler."

"How do you know that?"

Tim spoke as he walked. "'Cause that's what Slug's going to buy when he sells him."

"Sells him! He can't. He's not his. What about the horse's owner?"

Tim stopped and glared at Kim. "Did you see any ads lately for a lost horse?"

Kim shook her head.

"Exactly. I bet Holler never told the owner he lost the horse, and Slug knows it."

"But if Slug sells Wheeler, Holler will find out for sure."

"And beat the crap out of him."

"But Slug will beat Wheeler if he catches him!"

"And he'll beat *me* if he catches *me*!" Tim snapped.

Kim pleaded, "You have to help. You just have to."

Look," said Tim, his voice hard, "if that horse was in with the cows, it was going to the auction in Truro. Horses that end up there are being sold for *meat*."

"No!" Kim gasped.

"Yes. And as much as I hate that, I'm not risking my neck for some old broken-down nag."

"He's not a broken-down nag!" Kim choked. Tears flooded her eyes. "He's beautiful, really beautiful. Really!"

Tim softened and sighed. "All horses are beautiful when you have the Disease."

"This one *is*! Honest!"

"Sorry, Kim. I'd need an awfully good reason to mess with the meanest family in Meadow Green."

Kim took a deep, shuddering breath. She pulled out a pencil and drew on the side of the dumpster — a right-facing horse head, a left-facing horse head, two curved lines — and crossed the H.

"Is this a good reason?"

"The Hanoverian brand? So what?"

"It's on his left hip."

Tim looked at her blankly.

"It's on his left hip — right about there." She pointed to her thigh.

Tim blinked in disbelief. "No way."

"Yes way."

"Uh-uh. Can't be. No one sends a Hanoverian to a meat auction ... unless it's totally lame or totally psycho."

"Well he's *not* and someone *did* and Slug *will*!"

Tim stood quietly, thinking. At last he said, "Come on," and headed across the soccer field, keeping in line with the school's blind spot.

"You're going to miss school."

"And recess," he called back. "And, with luck, Slug. You coming?"

"But the school will call our parents. They'll want to know why we left."

"Jeez, I suddenly feel really sick, like maybe I'm going to throw up."

"You do?" asked Kim nervously.

Tim looked at her and rolled his eyes. Kim blushed. Tim had a talent for acting.

"I don't feel so good myself," she said as Tim strode away. She wasn't acting.

She pulled the bag off the dumpster, stuffed the whip into her knapsack. No way was it ever going to get back into Slug's hands. She'd bury it in the woods when she got home. She ran to catch up with Tim.

CHAPTER 17

The Rescue

"We can't walk all the way to Meadow Green," said Kim.

"My neighbor, Mr. Bell, is at Tim Hortons," Tim answered. "He usually heads home around 9:30."

"What if he's not there?"

"Oh, he'll be there. Never misses a day. Back when he was the snowplow driver, the clearest piece of road in Antigonish County in a blizzard was between Meadow Green and Tim Hortons. One time he even snuck out of the hospital right after surgery — couldn't live without his double double and cruller. They had to drag him back in an ambulance."

"He must really love the coffee," Kim said.

"Almost as much as the gossip. Keep your eyes open for a dark gray truck with red primer-paint sides."

They cut through the tiny subdivision, came out on the Trans-Canada near the traffic lights and jogged down the slope to Fast Food Alley.

A dark gray truck paused at the yield to the eastbound

lane. "Is that the truck?" asked Kim.

"Mr. Bell!" Tim shouted at the top of his lungs and waved. The driver, a ruddy, weathered man, leaned out and called, "What are you two doin' out of school?"

"Are you heading home?"

"Yupper."

Tim and Kim ran to the truck. "We need a ride," said Tim. "It's an emergency."

Mr. Bell chuckled. "A 911 emergency or a can't-stand-the-teacher emergency?"

"A horse emergency."

Mr. Bell sucked air through his teeth. "Get in," he said. "Something wrong with J.B.?"

"No. She's doing great. It's ... ah ... Kim's horse. This is Kim."

"Have we met?" Mr. Bell asked.

Kim scrunched against the door and shrugged.

"They bought Crackers' place," said Tim.

The driver nodded. "Yup, got the family look, all right."

All the way to Meadow Green, Tim and Mr. Bell traded horse stories, trying to one-up each other with the most colorful account. Kim could tell Mr. Bell's stories were all true — amazing but true. She wasn't so sure about Tim's.

Tim asked to be let off just past Mrs. MacLean's.

"You'll tell me what this is all about someday, eh?" said Mr. Bell.

"You've got an exclusive," Tim promised. They climbed out of the truck.

"Thanks," Kim whispered.

"You watch out for ghosts now," Mr. Bell said. Kim winced. His smile didn't match the earnest look in his eyes. He said to Tim, "Am I gonna get in trouble with your old man?"

"Only if you tell him that story about the dead horse one more time."

Loud guffaws bounded from the truck as it peeled away. Tim and Kim walked along the little road to the fish fence.

"You sure your dad's not fishing today?"

"Don't worry. He has to follow the schedule set by the Department of Fisheries. The river's only open for fishing at certain times. It's a shifting schedule. Lets some of the fish past the traps to spawn upriver. Dad's not fishing again till this afternoon."

They hiked over to the river pasture. The morning sun lifted soft scents from the grasses. A woodpecker drummed on the steel of the barn roof. Ghost's deep, throaty nicker came from the spruce copse. The dark horse stepped into the light and stood, head up, ears alert.

"Hi, Ghost," said Kim. "It's just me and Tim. Don't worry. Tim's okay."

Ghost lowered his head and sauntered over. He nuzzled Kim, hunting for an apple. "See? I told you he was beautiful."

"Lord liftin' lighthouses!" Tim exclaimed.

He walked around and around the horse, looking at him from every angle. He ran a hand down his neck, back and legs. He fingered the brand on Ghost's hip.

"Lord liftin' lighthouses!" he breathed again. "He's a

Hanoverian, all right. Even without the brand, you can tell he's a quality warmblood. Look at his conformation. His lines are perfect. Bet he moves like a dream."

"So what are we going to do?" asked Kim.

"We better find out who really owns this horse."

"But his real owner sent him for meat!"

"Impossible. Had to be a mistake," said Tim.

"What if it wasn't?"

"Kim," Tim said firmly, "it was a mistake. This is a Hanoverian. This is an expensive European horse. No one would send him to a meat auction on purpose. He's worth twenty times what he'd go for as meat! More!"

He stroked Ghost's shoulder. "Where'd you come from, big guy?"

"When I found him, he looked really awful. He was all plastered with cow manure."

"That's it!" said Tim. "There was a bunch of cows on Holler's truck, right?"

Kim nodded. "But —"

"And they were sold at auction. In May, right? Someone keeps track of who sells what. Mrs. MacLean will know how to find out who."

"But his owner doesn't deserve to get him back."

"Do you want Slug to have him?"

"No. But —"

"Do you have a better idea?"

I could keep him, Kim thought.

"Right. First we've got to get him out of here before Slug comes. We need a place to hide him. Anything in that old barn behind your house?"

"Just ghosts," Kim mumbled.

"Ghost," said Tim matter-of-factly. "There's just the one." He led the horse to the gate. "Great!" he barked. "Just great!"

A chain now bound the gate to the post — a chain with a padlock.

"Oh, no!" Kim cried. "That wasn't there the other day. This is the only way out."

Tim walked back and forth, muttering creative curses.

"There might be a way," he said. "Give me the bridle."

He slipped the bridle over Ghost's halter and faced the back end of the big horse. He put his left hand just above Ghost's withers, firmly grasping a handful of mane, and then in an elegant movement he flung his right leg up and over the horse's back. His body followed in a smooth arc. He landed just behind the withers, sat erect and collected the reins. Ghost tensed.

"Okay, big guy, let's see what you've got. Nice and easy."

They walked around the field, stopped, walked, turned, stopped, swung left, swung right, backed, walked fast, slow, sideways and then trotted. They trotted big circles and little circles, huge, long steps and short, bouncy steps. They halted near the gate.

Kim said, "Yesterday he didn't —"

"He's really well trained. Even better than J.B." Tim waved a hand toward the barn. "Haul three hay bales out and line them up."

Kim dragged over the lightest bales she could find.

Tim trotted Ghost toward the jump. The horse's ears pricked forward. He picked up speed and bounced over the hay. Tim signaled for a canter and, riding a large circle, they jumped three more times. On the last landing Tim pushed straight for the gate. Ghost took four big strides and lifted up, flying in a huge arc over the gate with air to spare. They slid to a stop on the other side.

"*Oh man!*" Tim cheered. "This horse has *wings!*"

Kim squeezed through the fence and threw her arms around Ghost's neck. "You were wonderful."

Tim slipped off Ghost. "No time for mushy stuff. Slug will be checking out the dumpsters any minute now. Getting his whip back might not satisfy him. He'll find out I'm not in school. He might guess where I went."

"How could he guess?"

"He thought the bridle was mine, remember? He thought it was me here with the horse. People like him get mean when they think you're messing with their property. Especially stolen property. My bet he shows up here. We better cover our tracks."

Kim agreed. There was a very good chance Slug would come — even if Kim hadn't kept the whip. No point in mentioning that to Tim. Slug was never getting his hands on the whip again and that was final.

"I'll go talk to Mrs. MacLean," said Tim. "See who sold those cows. You take the big guy to your place. Keep him in the water so you don't make any more tracks. I'll get the ones here." He stomped smooth the deep hoof-prints by the gate.

Kim pulled the reins over Ghost's head. She hesitated.

"Will you be okay?" asked Tim. "You know how to lead a horse, right?"

"Of course," said Kim. "It's just ... Ghost was in such bad shape. What if his owner doesn't want him back?"

Tim tapped his watch. "Let's worry about Slug first."

Kim sighed and led Ghost down the bank and into the cool current. He followed willingly, head up and curious. At the fish fence, he snorted and danced sideways up the bank. Kim rubbed his neck and crooned compliments, nudging him forward. He lifted his feet high over the tainted gravel as she coaxed him around fly-coated fish bits and back into the river.

They splashed slowly along, reveling in the heat of the sun and the chuckling water. Ghost stopped to drink, sucking noisily through pursed lips. He lifted his head, poked his nose at Kim and dribbled a lower lip full of water down her back. Kim squealed and laughed. Ghost snorted and pawed the river, flinging water in all directions.

"You're getting my bridle wet," Kim complained through her giggles. "Come on, you big oaf. We'll never get home at this rate."

As they turned up the blackberry path, a sudden uneasiness snatched at Kim like thorns on the arching canes. Behind them lay a private world of her and horse and water and sun. Ahead was the real world.

A jumbled wall of cloud marched over the sun. Determination marched through Kim. She would make sure Ghost didn't go back to the awful place he came from. She would make sure Tim understood.

Ghost gave her an impatient nudge. She looked into his deep brown eyes. "Don't worry. I won't let anyone hurt you ever again."

She led him up the path and across the field to the barn, glad its red bulk blocked the view from the house. She opened the back door and guided Ghost along the aisle and into the box stall.

"The perfect place to hide a horse," she whispered. She pulled off the bridle and closed the stall door. Ghost circled and whinnied anxiously.

"Shhh. Lunch is coming right up."

Kim hurried outside and quickly ripped up a huge armful of timothy grass that was growing thick and thigh-high behind the barn. Must have been an old manure pile here, she thought. She tossed the grass in the stall, then poked around the barn and found an old bucket caked with decades of dust.

"I'll clean this in the river and get you some water."

On the way, she looked for any tracks they might have left. Most of the ground was hard and unmarked. She found a hoof edge here, a toe dent there. She easily scuffed them away. Then she came to a complete hoofprint that took a little more effort to erase. Then another one farther along. She ground it flat and covered it with leaves.

Near the end of the path, two more complete tracks printed a patch of mud. One overlay the other. The one underneath was Ghost's. But over top was a gigantic hoofprint, more than twice the size of Ghost's.

Kim's pulse pounded in her ears. She suddenly remembered the huge hoofprint Gramma-Lou had been looking at in the river pasture. Only an enormous horse could make a print like that. There wasn't any horse that big around here ... anymore.

Nah. It was a trick of the light. It had to be. Maybe the huge print was just two prints side by side, looking like one. With her fingertip, Kim carefully traced the curve of the hoofprint — the uninterrupted curve.

An unlaced work boot stomped into the mud.

"Thanks for leaving those big tracks for me to follow."

CHAPTER 18

The Truth

"Thought you'd make a fool of me, eh?" Slug growled. "Do you think I'm stupid? You horse huggers are all alike. Trying to save some poor little horsey from the butcher. Well, that's what you think.

"WHERE'S MY HORSE?" he roared.

Kim turned to stone.

"Out of my way!" Slug pushed her aside and stormed up the path.

A cloud of blackflies struck at Kim. They crawled into her hair and under her shirt. One landed right on her eyeball. She jumped, as if awakened from a nightmare. She trailed after Slug, unable to stop herself, like a gawker sucked to the scene of a horrible accident.

Slug went straight to the barn. He threw open the back door, stomped inside and looked into the stall. "There you are, you black demon." As Kim staggered into view, he looked out and smiled a slow, cold smile. "Thanks for catching my horse, Runt."

He spied the bridle in the corner. He grabbed a rein and fought unsuccessfully to open the hook buckle attaching it to the bit. He pulled out a pocket knife and pressed it against the leather.

Kim gasped.

"So this isn't Tim's, it's yours." Slug smiled his ugliest smile. "Where's my whip?"

Kim fought not to glance down. Her knapsack sat at Slug's feet, the bulge of the whip almost touching his boot. She knew what he would do with that whip. She clenched her jaw.

"I'll cut it!" Slug bellowed.

Kim swallowed hard and glared. Slug sliced through the rein. Kim's heart stumbled. Slug grabbed the other rein. Kim tried to look away. The knife flashed. The reinless bridle fell to the floor.

Slug opened the stall door. Ghost backed up. Slug grabbed for his halter. The horse tossed his head. Slug lunged again. Ghost dodged, jaw tight, ears pinned flat. The whites of his eyes gleamed in the dim light.

"Stand still, you useless bastard!" Slug shouted.

Ghost wheeled around, head to the corner, hind-quarters bunched under and forward like a coiled spring. Slug cursed and swung the reins at Ghost's rump. Both hind hooves struck out, narrowly missing Slug's rib cage.

"I'll teach you to cross me!" Slug roared, and lashed the horse on the legs.

"Stop it! Stop it!" Kim screamed.

Slug struck Ghost again and again. The horse grunted

and threw himself up the back wall, trying to escape.

Kim dove for the knapsack. She ripped open the zipper, and her hand closed around the butt of the whip. She faced the stall, heart drumming, muscles rigid.

Her voice vibrated — like the shake of a rattler's tail. She bit out each word. "Get away from that horse."

Slug flicked her a snarling glance and turned back to the horse. Ghost's sides heaved. The damp scent of sweat poured from the stall.

"I said, GET AWAY FROM THAT HORSE!"

Slug almost laughed. Then he saw the whip. A twisted smile curled his lips. "Thanks. I can use that." He stepped forward.

The world suddenly dropped into slow motion. Kim saw her arm rise, the lash of the whip unfurl with elegant beauty. Her arm came down hard and fast. The lash tip licked toward Slug and vanished. A gigantic crack ripped the air. Blood trickled from Slug's left cheek.

Slug went white, then rage red.

Kim flicked the whip handle up. The lash coiled obediently at her feet. She seethed. "Get out."

Slug's mouth contorted. He took one step back.

Sweat itched down Kim's back. She lifted the whip high. "GET OUT!"

Slug backed another step. "I'll get you for this."

Thunder thumped in the distance like a fearful heart. A childlike voice sang out. "Domino. I saw you, Domino. Where are you?" Gramma-Lou appeared in the doorway, wearing Colm's green bathrobe — inside out.

"Is that you, Lynn?"

Kim kept her eyes glued on Slug. "Gramma-Lou, you should go back to the house."

"Lynn, where's Domino?"

"He's not here," Kim answered firmly. "Please go back to the house."

Gramma-Lou went to Slug. She stood between him and Kim. She put her hands on either side of Slug's face.

"Did you see Domino?"

Slug jerked back. Gramma-Lou's right hand came away covered in blood. A low moan rose as she wiped her hand on the robe — red on green. She looked at the dirt floor and lifted each foot as if to avoid stepping in something. "Blood," she whimpered. "Puddles of blood."

"She's nuts," said Slug.

"She is not!"

"Yes, she is. She's crackers, just like her father."

"Shut up."

Gramma-Lou started to cry.

"It's okay, Gramma-Lou. It's okay."

"No," Gramma-Lou moaned. "You weren't there."

"I wasn't where?"

A black chuckle sprang from Slug. "She was there." He took a step toward them. "She knows."

Kim's knuckles whitened on the whip. "Get back."

He retreated, but pushed with his voice. "Folks say her father hated farming so much it drove him insane. Just went to the barn one day and blew the brains out of everything that moved." He looked at Gramma-Lou. "You remember, don't you?"

He lifted an invisible rifle to his shoulder. "He blew the brains out of the cows first. BAM! BAM! BAM! BAM!"

"No, he didn't!" shouted Kim.

Slug smiled darkly. "Then he picked off the cats. KAPOW! Then blew the heads off the chickens."

Gramma-Lou's face was leaden.

He leered at her. "I'm right, aren't I?" His words dripped with malice. "Then he killed the *horses.*"

"Stop it! That's not true!" Kim felt sick to her stomach. The thunder rumbled overhead now, on and on. It started to rain heavily — a panicky pounding on the roof.

Gramma-Lou said in a small, tight voice, almost unheard under the rain. "He wouldn't stop screaming."

"See? She remembers. Bet she screamed, too." His gaze twitched between Gramma-Lou, Kim and the whip.

"Shot them over and over," he continued. "Till there was blood dripping from the rafters."

Kim couldn't help but glance upward. Slug took two quick steps toward her. Kim flinched the whip upward. "I'll use it again!" she screamed. This time Slug stood his ground.

The rain stopped as suddenly as it started. A car pulled up outside. Two doors thumped.

"You're lying!" said Kim. "Gramma-Lou's father sold the horses. He never killed them. He never killed anything."

"I'm afraid he did," said Erika softly.

She and Tim stepped into the barn. Erika took Gramma-Lou's arm. "Come, dear heart, you shouldn't be in here."

Gramma-Lou refused to be moved.

Slug lunged for the whip. Tim jumped in front of Kim. "Back off!" he yelled.

"What's going on in here?" Colm rushed in the door. Lightning strobed the barn. A brutal crack shattered the air. Ghost snorted anxiously.

"Where the hell did that horse come from?" Colm barked.

"Your kid stole my horse," answered Slug.

"He's not your horse," Kim growled. "He escaped from your father's truck."

"Are you Holler's boy?" asked Colm.

"Yes, sir."

Colm pulled out his cell phone. "What's your father's number?"

"Ah, Dad's probably not home. I'll just take the horse and go."

"But it's not his horse!" cried Kim.

"What's your number?" Colm repeated — an order, not a question.

Slug mumbled something. Colm punched in the number, cursed at his phone and stepped outside to get a better signal. He returned shortly. "He'll be right over."

"You can't let him take Ghost!" Kim gasped. "He'll have him killed!"

Lightning flashed again. Thunder thumped into the distance.

Gramma-Lou started to sob. "He killed them. I tried to stop him. He killed them all."

"Who's been telling her those awful stories?" asked

Colm angrily. He hovered around his mother, hands fluttering over her shoulders but never landing.

"No one had to tell her," said Erika. "She remembered."

Ghost snorted and pawed the stall door.

"It's that goddamn horse," said Colm. "It's got her all worked up. Goddamn horses ruin everything."

"NO!" said Gramma-Lou with sudden sharpness. She looked Colm straight in the eye. "*Fathers ruin everything.*"

CHAPTER 19

The Trade

Gramma-Lou's eyes were clear, as if her tears had washed the clouds from her mind. It was the old Gramma-Lou. Kim's Gramma-Lou.

"He tried to kill him. There was so much blood," she said to Erika, her voice cracking. "I took him. I took him and I *ran.*"

"Sometimes running is the right thing to do," said Erika.

"What kind of gibberish is she talking?" Colm demanded.

Erika got that somewhere-else, somewhen-else look again. "We heard the gunshots from our place," she said in a thin, flat tone. "There was a gigantic rainstorm. At first we thought the noise we heard was thunder. Then Lou and Domino galloped into the yard through the pouring rain. They were both splattered with blood. Lou's socks were red to her ankles. It was awful. So awful. Lou's father shot all the animals. He tried to kill Domino, too, but she ran away with him. She begged us to hide him from her father. We did."

Erika opened her arms, reaching across more than half a century to her old friend. They clung to each other.

"She never ... told me," said Colm.

"I don't think she ever told herself," said Erika softly. "You were so brave, Lou. You saved him."

"Yes. I saved them both."

"That's right. You did."

"Both?" asked Colm. "What does she mean 'both'?"

"She saved Domino from her father," said Erika. "And you from yours."

"Saved me?"

"He tried to kill you," said Erika simply.

"That's garbage! You're both crazy! Dad loved me! We were happy in Dartmouth. If you hadn't taken us away ... if she hadn't ever seen that horse farm — I'd still have a father."

Gramma-Lou released Erika. She said to Colm, "I needed a job."

Colm bristled. "I needed a father!"

She shook her head. "You don't remember."

"I remember all right. I remember you loved those goddamn horses more than Dad — more than *me*."

Gramma-Lou reached up and touched the zigzag scar on his cheek. "Do you remember this?"

Colm shrugged away her hand. "I ... I fell down."

"Where?"

"What difference does it make?"

She barely whispered, as if afraid to hear the words spoken aloud. "Your father did that."

"My father would never —"

"You were only four. He told you not to touch his baseball. But you did anyway. He threw you down the stairs."

"He did not! That's bullshit!"

No one moved. Even the barn seemed to hold its breath. The only sound was the rhythmic plink of water dripping from the eves. A large truck rumbled up the driveway.

"That's my dad," Slug muttered.

"Right," said Colm. "Bring that horse outside."

"It's not his horse!" Kim insisted. "Erika and Tim are going to find out who owns him."

"We did," said Tim apologetically. "He belongs to Holler."

"That can't be."

"Afraid it is," said Tim. "When the horse ran away, the owner wouldn't pay Holler his trucking fee. He said if Holler found the horse, he could keep it."

Janis appeared in the doorway. "There's a man out here looking for a horse. I said he had the wrong place."

"For christ's sake!" Colm rushed outside. Everyone followed.

Holler stood beside his shiny black crew-cab pickup. He was built like a fire hydrant, with a face almost as red and a flattened nose that looked permanently pressed against a windowpane.

"Hold on, Mr., ah, I never got your last name," said Colm.

"Beaton," Holler replied, ignoring Colm's outstretched hand. "Where's my horse?"

"I'm sorry. My girl took your horse from your son."

Holler turned on Slug. "*You* had the horse?"

Slug's eyes darted around as if looking for an escape. He didn't find one.

"For how long?" Holler shouted.

"It's gained lots of weight," said Slug. "It'll get a better price now."

"You useless bastard! I needed that money last month."

"But you said you'd buy me a four-wheeler with that money."

"That horse isn't worth a rat's ass, let alone a four-wheeler!"

"But you promised! It's *my* money!"

"Shut up, you useless ..." And he slapped Slug hard across the face.

"Look here," said Colm. "Just take the horse and leave."

"No!" Kim exclaimed.

Holler glanced over and saw the whip in her hand. "Is that my whip?" He glared at Slug, his voice as hard as a punch. "You hide that, too?"

True terror bleached Slug's face. For the first time, Kim saw him as a boy — just a fifteen-year-old boy, tall, underweight, with clothes that hadn't been washed this month and the expression of a dog about to be beaten. Her hand tightened on the whip. She heard herself say, "This is my whip."

"Sure looks like mine," Holler hissed.

Kim was too afraid to even blink. On the soft edge of her vision, she saw Janis straighten and say, "You've seen one whip, you've seen them all."

Gramma-Lou put her arm around Kim's shoulder. "Go home," she ordered, as if talking to a stray.

Holler glared at the women. He spat into the gravel and turned to Colm. "Where's my horse?"

"No, Colm. Please," Kim gasped. "You can't let him take the horse. He'll be killed!"

Holler huffed. "As if you care. You people shoot horses."

"Janis, please! Don't let him —"

Janis brushed a blond strand from Kim's forehead with feather lightness. Then she turned to Holler and asked, "How much is the horse worth?"

Kim couldn't believe her ears.

Surprise and cunning played across Holler's unshaven features. "It goes to an auction. Never know what I could get."

"I'm sure you have a good idea," said Janis.

Colm caught Janis's intent. "Oh no you don't. The last thing we need is a goddamn horse."

Janis didn't even look at him. "But it's the first thing Kim needs." Janis's voice was as hard and solid as a bolted steel door. "That ... and a father who'd know it's the first thing she needs if he ever took the time to look. Or do you want her to grow up hating her father like you hate your mother?"

Kim's jaw dropped. Who was this woman?

Colm turned crimson, his scar in bright relief. Gramma-Lou's hand went to her cheekbone. Colm caught the movement out of the corner of his eye. His hand reflexively mirrored hers, then closed into a fist. His teeth ground as if chewing on words he desperately wanted to speak. His fist slowly uncurled.

"How much for that goddamn horse?" he asked Holler.

Kim could barely breathe.

"A thousand ..." Holler paused, looking for a reaction. He got none. "And a half."

"You just said he wasn't worth a rat's ass," said Erika, "and you won't get more than eight hundred from the meat buyers."

Holler grumbled. "Twelve hundred. That's final."

Colm spread his hands in honest helplessness. "I don't have that kind of money," he said to Janis.

"You have to buy him!" Kim pleaded. "You have to!"

"This horse is, ah ..." Tim fumbled for the right words. "He's in pretty bad shape, and he could be completely wild and untrainable, or nasty, or lame. Hard to say. Could be he's not worth a penny more than meat — and he's still pretty thin. I'll give you three hundred for him."

"Humph," Holler protested. "A thousand dollars. Absolute lowest."

"Janis, Colm, pleeease!"

Colm flinched. "Still too much," he said, almost gently. "I just don't have it."

No one noticed Gramma-Lou go over to the bird feeder. She returned, picked up Slug's hand and placed Colm's baseball on his palm. She folded his fingers tightly around it.

"Even-steven," she said.

"My baseball!" Colm exclaimed. He lunged at Slug.

Gramma-Lou stepped between them, warding off Colm.

"But that's my baseball!" Colm protested. "The one that Father gave to me."

Gramma-Lou looked up at him, shaking her head. "That's not true."

Colm flushed. His jaw worked under his beard. "Mother," he said, barely controlling his impatience, "that's the baseball Father gave me — the day you took me away."

"You stole that ball."

Colm rolled his eyes. "Mother. I never —"

"He said he'd come for you. You were smarter than me — you didn't believe him."

Colm's brow creased. "Mother ..."

"You took his baseball. I saw you. You hid it in your boot."

Colm stared at her for what seemed like forever.

"Blue boots with yellow trim," Gramma-Lou whispered.

Colm blinked. The color drained from his face. He looked down at his feet. He teetered like a man on a precipice, about to fall. He gasped in a breath. Three words leaked out in a tiny voice. "He didn't come."

Holler snapped, "Look here. I got work to do."

Gramma-Lou replied calmly, "The ball for the horse."

"Are you out of your skull?" Holler asked.

Slug laughed. "What do I want with this old thing?"

Gramma-Lou tapped the ball with one large-knuckled finger. "Words," she said.

Slug scowled. He rolled the baseball over. His lips moved as he read.

"Jesus, Mary and Joseph!" he shouted. "A Babe Ruth baseball! A Babe Ruth baseball!" He suddenly frowned. "This ain't for real."

"Darn right it is," said Janis, "and it's a good trade."

"A baseball for a horse?" Holler snorted. "You people think we're stupid around here?"

"My husband once said that ball would sell on eBay for at least two thousand dollars, didn't you, Colm? And just last week on TV, I heard that big-name baseballs are very collectible. CEOs put them on their desks."

"Is that right, Slugger?" asked Holler.

"A Babe Ruth baseball. You bet! Hell, yes!" said Slug. "What year is it?"

"1934," said Janis.

Slug stared at the ball. "This is a million times better than my Duke Snider card — than all my baseball cards put together!"

"I don't know," said Holler suspiciously.

"Well, you could always take the horse," said Janis. "And it could kick your trailer apart and run away again."

Holler snarled, "Keep the stinking nag. Slugger, get your useless butt in the truck."

Slug climbed into the truck next to his father. He said to Kim, "Your grandmother's crazy. You're all crazy."

Holler's truck roared away, tires spitting gravel and mud.

Kim hugged her grandmother with all her might. "You were brilliant, Gramma-Lou!" Then she threw her arms around Janis. "Thank you. Thank you. Thank you."

"Don't thank me. It was Colm's ball."

Kim went to Colm and hugged him. "Thanks, Dad," she whispered.

Colm patted her absentmindedly on the back of the head. "I shouldn't have let you make me do that. My baseball was worth way more than that rat's ass, as Holler put it."

"Then I'm getting myself some rats!" Tim crowed. "'Cause around here, a rat's ass is worth over ten grand!"

CHAPTER 20

The Fence

"Who are you?" asked Colm. "What are you talking about?"

"Tim Ritland. That was a real good deal you just made, sir."

"How's that? You said that horse was mean and lame!"

Tim laughed. "I only said it *might* be."

"He's a Hanoverian!" said Kim.

"Who? Tim?"

"No. My horse!"

Kim gasped. The two words she had dreamed of saying all her life had just slipped out so easily. Her eyes met Gramma-Lou's. Gramma-Lou nodded and smiled.

"My horse," Kim said slowly, savoring the exquisite flavor of each word, "is an honest-for-real Hanoverian. With a Hanoverian brand. All the way from Germany!"

"He's a real gentleman," said Tim, "and he's beautifully trained. You should see him jump!"

"This doesn't make any sense," said Colm. "How did

a German hanowhatsit end up with a bunch of cows on the way to the meat market?"

"I phoned Willy Dan Ian," said Ericka. "He works at the sales barn. He said everyone remembered the load of cows that almost got away because of some crazy horse. They belonged to a Mr. Hyland Miller in Baddeck. So I called him, and he was more than happy to tell me his end of the story. He said a German fellow with a bunch of horses owed him for three years' worth of hay. When Miller demanded payment, he woke up one morning to find a horse tied to his gate post and the German's property abandoned. Skipped the country, leaving nothing but debts ... and that horse. Mr. Miller was pretty angry at being stuck with another mouth to feed. He obviously never realized what a valuable animal he had — the German had more than paid his bill. Mr. Miller said the horse spent the winter chasing his cows, so he shipped him with the culls in the spring. You know the rest."

Gramma-Lou shook her head. "Tsk, tsk, tsk."

"Is that horse really worth ten thousand dollars?" asked Colm.

"More!" said Tim.

"Only if you sell him," Kim exclaimed with sudden fear. "And you're not going to sell him!"

"We can't afford a horse!" Colm whined. "People charge big money to board horses."

"We can keep him here," said Kim.

"Not on your life. I'm not getting stuck hauling water to the barn at 6:00 AM in the middle of winter."

"I'll haul all the water. Honest I will! I can take care

of him. Gramma-Lou taught me how. Gramma-Lou can help, too. Won't you, Gramma-Lou?"

Gramma-Lou's expression brightened. "Posolutely," she said.

"She doesn't know what you're talking about," said Colm.

"Horses, of courses," said Gramma-Lou.

"Well, Colm," said Janis, "horses do seem to be good medicine for your mother."

"Expensive medicine. And you can't keep a horse without a fence. That's more money. And I damn well don't have the time to build one."

"I can help," said Tim.

Colm ignored him. "And then there's feed and needles and shoes and —"

Tim interrupted again. "He might not need shoes. He has great feet. And I've got an idea about the fence."

Colm glared at Tim.

"I can help pay for it," said Janis. "The new call center just bought three of my new paintings for their foyer."

"What? *Your* paintings?" Colm looked truly puzzled.

Janis smiled — a crisp, confident smile.

"You never told me," said Colm.

"You never asked."

"How much are they going to pay?"

"E-nough," said Janis, emphasizing both syllables, with that bright, fierce look in her eye that said enough money *and* enough questions.

Colm threw up his hands. "Oh, do whatever you want. Just don't expect me to have anything to do with it." He looked at his watch. "Look what you've done! You've made me late! I'm supposed to give a school tour at eleven."

Tim watched him leave and said calmly, "He doesn't happen to work in the university's biology department, does he?"

"Yes," said Janis.

"Guess I missed the tour, too." He shrugged. "Oh well, you've been on one field trip, you've been on them all." He grinned. "Besides, I've got something better to do. Kim, you going to be home this afternoon?"

Kim looked at Janis. Janis nodded.

"Right," said Tim. "I'll see you in a little bit."

"Do you need a drive home?" asked Erika.

"Nah, I'm not going that far," said Tim, and he headed up the driveway.

The sun broke through the fleeing clouds. A shaft of light caressed the barn roof, lifting steam from the black tar patches. The air hung thick with cool, earthy sweetness.

"Just us women left," said Janis.

"And my horse," said Kim. She giggled. "My horse. My horse. My horse." She felt as if she was going to explode with joy. "Want to see my horse? I'll take him out."

"Are you sure it's safe?" asked Janis. "I mean, he's so big."

"Bigger's not always better," said Gramma-Lou.

Erika chuckled and took her old friend's arm. "That's not what you used to say. We'd love to see your horse, Kim. What are you going to call him?"

"I've been calling him Ghost."

Erika tucked back a loose lock of hair. "Ghost? Why did you call him that?"

Kim reddened. "Well," she mumbled, "you said the black horse was dead. But I saw a horse for sure. And everyone talked about a ghost so ... when I found a real horse, I called him Ghost."

"My, my," said Erika.

"Well, I'd like to meet your Ghost," said Janis.

~

Kim spent the rest of the morning in heaven. Janis and Erika set up lawn chairs in the shade and talked while Kim held Ghost's lead rope as he grazed and Gramma-Lou sat in the grass weaving chains of dandelions into necklaces and crowns. They both giggled with glee when Ghost thought his crown tasted better than it looked. Then Kim and Gramma-Lou brushed Ghost until his soft gloss turned to a bright shine. Gramma-Lou braided the sticky-up bits of Ghost's mane down into the rest so it would all lie neat and flat against his neck. Gramma-Lou was almost her old self and talked about how her mother planted the elm tree beside the barn, the time Ricky caught the biggest trout in the river and the hot days haying and the cool days digging potatoes.

At noon Kim put Ghost in the barn, and they all went in for lunch. Gramma-Lou almost fell asleep in her egg sandwich. Janis helped her up to bed. As Janis was coming back downstairs, Mr. Bell's primer-red pickup pulled around behind the house. A van drove in after it.

"Now who can that be?" asked Janis. They stepped outside to see Tim jump out of the truck and Lana, Margaret, Michelle and Mike clamber from the van.

"Ladies," said Tim with a flourish, "meet the Meadow Green Fencers."

"Hi!" said the other four in harmony. Then Lana said, "Our field trip finished early so we got the afternoon off. Tim called just as we were heading to Hug a Horse."

"I was heading home," said Mike.

"What's all this?" asked Janis, looking at the pile of lumber in the back of Mr. Bell's truck.

"It's a fence," said Tim, as if it wasn't perfectly obvious.

"I don't know if I can afford this," said Janis nervously.

"It's *free!*' said Tim, grinning from ear to ear. "Besides, we're doing Mr. Bell a favor. All this stuff's been collecting dust in his barn ever since his horse died five years ago."

"Not just dust," Michelle whined. "Icky cobwebs!"

"This is Mr. Bell," said Tim, introducing the driver of the truck. "And that's Lana's mom." He waved toward the van.

"Nice to meet you," called Lana's mom. "I've got to get back to work. Lana, I'll be here at five." She backed up and drove away.

Janis shook Mr. Bell's hand. "Hi, I'm Janis O'Connor. Surely you must want some money for all this."

"Oh, I got more than money can buy," said Mr. Bell. "I got a firsthand account of 'the Great Horse Trade.' The best horse story around here in decades!"

Tim cupped his hand over one side of his mouth and said semi-secretly, "And they're going to hear it at Tim Hortons for decades."

Janis asked again, "Are you positive you won't take anything for it?"

"We'll take some milk and cookies," said Tim.

"Chocolate ones!" shouted Lana.

Janis laughed. "I think I can manage that. Mr. Bell, would you like to come in for tea? Erika, you're staying, too, of course." The women led Mr. Bell into the house.

"Hey, Shrimp," Tim barked to Kim. "Lend a hand." Kim blushed and ran over to help drag fence posts off the tailgate.

"First things first," said Michelle. "Let's get the *real* story."

"Then we have to see the horse!" said Lana.

"I told you the real story," said Tim.

"You told us Kim slashed Slug's face with a bull whip," said Lana, throwing her hands in the air. "Like we're going to believe that. And that her grandmother traded an old baseball for a purebred Hanoverian."

It did sound impossible, thought Kim. She barely believed it herself. She swallowed and said in a small voice, "I did. She did."

"You mean Tim didn't exaggerate?" Michelle exclaimed in disbelief.

"I never exaggerate," said Tim. "Now let's get this stuff off the truck before it collapses under the weight."

Margaret looked troubled. "Does that mean ... the story about Crackers is true? Kim's great-grandfather really shot his horses? And they still ... haunt this place?"

"Haunt, shmaunt," said Lana brightly. "You can't believe everything Tim says."

But Margaret was deeply serious. "Imagine having a father like that."

Kim hadn't until now. And didn't want to.

They all got back to unloading the fence posts, rolls of electric fence wire and tools onto the grass. Then Kim led them to the barn. Everyone oohed and aahed over Ghost. Even Mike, who knew only dairy cows, thought Ghost was pretty impressive.

"What's his name?" asked Margaret.

"I call him Ghost," said Kim.

"Aren't ghosts supposed to be white?" asked Michelle.

"He's so amazing," said Lana. "When I have lots of money, I'm going to buy a Hanoverian."

"Have you been on him yet?" asked Michelle.

Kim blushed again. She wasn't about to tell the truth about falling off and get laughed at. "I don't have a saddle," she said quietly.

"I think Vanessa has an old one that might fit," said Tim. "She might loan it until you can buy your own."

"How old do you think he is?" asked Margaret.

Kim shrugged.

"Bet Tim knows," said Lana. "Tim knows everything." That was clearly said to annoy him. It didn't.

Tim pushed Ghost's lips apart and peered at his huge yellowed teeth. "See that hook there? And those blackish dents?"

"Is that good?" asked Mike.

"Real good. He's only seven. Good for another hundred thousand miles. Now let's get some work done around here."

The fence went together like magic. Tim and Mike were deadly with the heavy mauls — the fence posts didn't stand a chance. They bit into the ground, one after the other, in crisp, straight lines.

Tim directed the work, planning the fence so Ghost could come and go freely from the barn. The girls all took orders well, except for Lana, who kept telling jokes that made everyone laugh so hard they couldn't lift a hammer.

In mid-afternoon, Janis, Erika and Mr. Bell came out to see how the work was going. Janis brought fresh cinnamon biscuits, double fudge brownies and orange juice. "I hope this is okay. I'm not sure what you kids like. Kim never has friends over." Everyone assured her it was more than okay and cleaned off the tray in under two minutes.

"Where's your grandmother?" Michelle asked Kim. "Bet she has tons of good horse stories."

Janis answered for Kim. "She's asleep. Though god knows how anyone could sleep through the noise of this crowd. But if you want stories, ask Mr. Bell."

Mr. Bell chuckled. "We'll come out and inspect the fence when you're done."

Mike got started on a gate for the front corner of the barn using old planks he found inside. Lana and Kim finished nailing the electric fence keepers to the posts, and Margaret and Michelle strung the white electric wire. By four thirty the fence was complete. Tim plugged in the electric fence and tested it by touching it with a shovel. Sparks snapped off the wire.

Kim went into the barn to get Ghost. Her cheeks hurt from smiling. She didn't know having friends could feel this good: The fence was complete. She hadn't said anything stupid all afternoon. She didn't get laughed at. And she even got most of Lana's jokes.

She let Ghost out of the box stall, where he had been anxiously pacing. He trotted around inspecting his new boundaries, then burst into the air in a volley of kicks and bucks that awed his audience.

Applause rang out. It was Gramma-Lou. Erika and Janis joined in.

Michelle asked Gramma-Lou, "Did you ever see such a nice horse, Mrs. O'Connor?"

Gramma-Lou's brow crinkled. "Do you know Mama?" she replied. Then she saw Kim and smiled. "Hi, Lynn."

Kim felt all eyes on her. Her face grew hot. Her stomach knotted. "Hi," she whispered.

Gramma-Lou looked around and whispered back, "Where's Mama?"

Kim chewed her lip. She knew everyone must think her grandmother was as crazy as Crackers. What else could they think? Could she tell them the truth? What if she told them Gramma-Lou had Alzheimer's? Would that change anything?

And how would Gramma-Lou feel?

Kim suddenly wondered if anyone had told Gramma-Lou. She knew Janis wouldn't. And Colm certainly hadn't. She looked helplessly at her grandmother.

Janis cleared her throat and said softly, "Lou, would you like some brownies? Double fudge."

Gramma-Lou's eyes lit up. "Mmmm!"

Janis led her mother-in-law indoors, followed by Erika and her cane. Mr. Bell blew out a breath. "Well," he said, "the fence passes inspection. My job's done. I'm beat. I think I'll be getting home. You coming, Tim?"

"Your job! Yeah, your jaw muscles must be exhausted!" Tim exclaimed, wiping his sweaty face on his shirt. "I'm done, too, I guess. Come on, Mike. See you, Kim."

The girls hung around watching the grazing horse. No one spoke. Wood frogs called for mates from their wet holes near the river, croaking, croaking, croaking in rhythm with the horse's grinding teeth. Just before five, Lana's mother pulled up in the van.

"See ya tomorrow, Kim," said Lana.

Margaret smiled. "Yeah, only two more days of school!"

"Plus grading day next week," Michelle corrected. "Bye, Kim."

When Colm came home, the first thing he saw was the fence. "How in the name of god did you get that done in one afternoon?"

Kim answered, "My friends came over." The words "my friends" tasted nearly as good on her lips as "my horse."

"Hmm. How much did it cost?" Colm asked.

"Not a cent," Janis answered. She winked at Kim, then wiggled a finger in one ear. "But I paid for it twenty times over."

Gramma-Lou smiled brightly over supper. She talked very little but made herself understood each time. Janis said the horse had definitely been good medicine for her, so when Gramma-Lou broke the second plate trying to help with the dishes, Janis suggested Kim take her out to see Ghost.

As Kim closed the new gate behind them, Gramma-Lou got very agitated. Kim tried to steer her back to the house, afraid the barn had stirred up more bad memories.

Gramma-Lou stopped her and said in a frightened voice, "Kim, I don't remember leaving PEI."

"You and Janis came on the ferry, on Saturday."

"Oh," said Gramma-Lou, "that's right." She remained quiet for a few minutes and then said, "I get confused. What's wrong with me, Kim?"

Kim didn't know what to say, so she repeated Janis's words. "That happens to everyone when they get older. It's okay."

But it wasn't okay. It wasn't the truth.

Gramma-Lou looked hard at Kim. "Are you sure?"

Kim's throat tightened. Anxious tears welled up. She said huskily, "You have Alzheimer's, Gramma-Lou."

Gramma-Lou's face softened. She nodded. "So this is bye-bye Lou time?"

No! Kim wanted to shout. No. The tears poured down her cheeks. "Yes," Kim whispered.

They stood quietly for a long time. Ghost wandered over. Gramma-Lou smiled and rubbed him under the jaw. Kim took Gramma-Lou's hand. They walked to the elm tree and curled up at its base and watched Ghost graze. Calmness settled with the dew. They sat there until the planets glowed brighter than the western sky.

"Time for bed," Kim said at last.

Gramma-Lou smiled. "He waited for me."

Kim almost asked "Who?" when she realized she knew. She had known for a long time. The huge hoofprints, the side-by-side paths in the dew of the river pasture, the golden movements in the corner of her eye, the dreams.

Domino.

"Yes, he did," she whispered.

They went into the house hand in hand. Gramma-Lou called Janis a nice lady and thanked her for her help. Kim went to her quiet green bedroom, curled up and slept.

～

All around, the confusion of rain continued — except there in the center. On a warm hug of extra-green grass under an extra-blue June sky stood the huge golden horse, calmly grazing. On his back his diminutive passenger lay asleep, a blissful smile on her lips.

CHAPTER 21

The Homecoming

Kim awoke knowing that something was missing. She felt like one of Janis's unfinished paintings, where details of fat-leafed sea peas, glistening sandbars and cloud-piled sky framed a primer-white blankness. She felt as if there was no ocean where the ocean should be.

Kim jumped out of bed. A soft drizzle hissed against the windows. She trotted downstairs and through the house. Janis was humming in the shower. The water pipes rumbled in tune with Colm's snoring. Kim walked softly into her grandmother's bedroom. "Rise and shine, Gramma-Lou."

Her grandmother didn't stir. She lay peacefully, a blissful smile on her lips. Kim touched her cheek. It was cold.

The doctor said it was her heart. She had died quietly during the night.

Janis said it was the best way to go.

Colm said nothing.

Kim cried an ocean of tears. For days, if it wasn't for Ghost, she wouldn't have gotten out of bed. Later she remembered hugging him, pressing her face against his warm furry comfort and clinging desperately when the sadness buckled her knees.

At some point Erika offered to help arrange the wake and funeral.

"There will be no wake," said Janis with an authority Kim had never heard before. "Lou didn't want the nosy and the curious gawking at her old bones. She wanted to be cremated and have her ashes sprinkled over the river pasture in Meadow Green. I used to wonder how I was going to get permission to do such a thing — until we moved here. Strange how things work out."

"It doesn't matter what she wanted," said Colm. "We'll have a regular wake and funeral. That's how it's done around here. People need to pay their respects."

"What people? Erika is the only one who didn't think of Lou as just the daughter of a madman."

"I'm sure there are others. What about the people I work with?"

"NO!" said Janis — the new Janis. "It's all in her will."

"My lawyer better have a look at this will of hers," said Colm. "The government'll take most of everything if a will's not done right, if it's not legal."

"You want to spend money on a lawyer, you go right

ahead. But Lou's will is legal. And as her executor, I'm going to see that her wishes are carried out. She will be cremated, and everything she owned goes in a trust for Kim. As simple as that."

And, amazingly, it was. Colm never said another word about it. He refused to take off the five days of compassionate leave allowed him and went to work. Janis said he was just hiding in his office. She, in turn, hid in her studio.

By the end of the week, Kim stopped crying long enough to go and see what Janis wanted for lunch. She found the studio door wide open and Janis smiling. "I'd like you to see what I've been working on." She stood back from a huge circular canvas, as wide as Kim was tall.

Instead of Janis's usual meticulous brush strokes, broad sweeps of paint colored the canvas. The old darkness lingered only in intended shadows. Light pounded down on a wild sky full of birds dancing over crashing waves and stoic dunes. But the heart of the painting glowed with a soul-soaring peace in the form of a periwinkle blue cottage.

Kim just stood there, lips pressed into a tight grin, tears pouring down.

"I guess you like it," said Janis softly. She folded Kim into her arms and they rocked with the waves and the wind till the seabirds quieted both their tears.

"Mr. Cameron and Lillian are coming over for the ceremony tomorrow," said Janis. "Is there something special you'd like to do? Something Gramma-Lou would have liked?"

Tomorrow was Saturday already? Kim sighed. She pictured the river pasture, the old barn and sloping green field ... and an idea lit up inside her like sunlight on a rainbow.

"I know exactly what Gramma-Lou would like." And told her.

"Do you want me to come with you?" asked Janis.

"Yes. But I think I can do this myself."

"Gramma-Lou would be very proud of you."

Kim biked to Hug a Horse. It was Friday, grocery day. Tim was in charge. He and the four girls were working in the barn. They all said hi — and all looked uncomfortable. It was Patsy who said "Sorry to hear about your grandmother."

"Thanks," said Kim. She turned to Tim. Better ask before she lost her nerve. "Tim," she said, "I have an idea." On the way over, she had thought of fifteen ways to tell him her idea, but only one was the truth.

"My grandmother loved horses. She had the Disease, too," Kim explained. "She wanted her ashes spread in the river pasture. The ceremony is tomorrow afternoon and I want to spread her ashes ... from horseback."

"That's cool," said Tim.

"Problem is," Kim continued hesitantly, "problem is I can't ride Ghost. I tried." She chewed her lip. "I ... I fell off." No one said anything. No one laughed.

Kim took a deep breath. "But I can ride Jelly Bean better. And I thought of how good Ghost went for you. And I thought maybe you would let me ride Jelly Bean tomorrow for my grandmother and then, um, maybe ... well, we could sort of switch horses for the summer."

"Are you serious?"

Kim remembered how she had always told herself if she ever owned a horse she would never let anyone near it. Now she owned a beautiful Hanoverian and had just offered to trade him for a spotty pony. She nodded. "But you have to teach me how to ride J.B."

"Heck, yes!" said Tim. "Are you sure? Ghost will have to stay here."

Kim nodded again.

"It's a deal!" said Tim. "J.B. will love it at your place."

Kim smiled. It felt good to smile again.

On Saturday morning, Mr. Cameron and Lillian arrived. The sight of Lillian's green hatchback, the car that had so often ferried Kim and Gramma-Lou to the grocery store, started Kim sobbing again. And her old friends looked so different. Mr. Cameron's bald head was balder and his thin frame thinner. Lillian's hips had gained what her uncle had lost, and her hair had silvered slightly. Lillian hugged Kim hard, sharing tears.

Mr. Cameron took his turn with a solid embrace. "There, there," he crooned. "How's my little helper with the magic touch?" He nudged her cheeks into a smile with his calloused thumbs. "How 'bout you show me this new horse of yours?"

Kim led them to the barn, where Ghost was hiding from the day's flies. When she said he was a purebred Hanoverian and could jump really high, Mr. Cameron told her Hanoverians were originally bred as carriage horses. "If it ain't part cart horse, it ain't no good," he said, nodding his approval.

Tim showed up a few minutes later. Kim had asked him to come over after Mr. Cameron and Lillian arrived. That way, Janis had suggested, if Colm didn't like the horse trade, he couldn't make a scene. He didn't, just grumbled that he didn't trade his most prized possession so some other kid could ride the best horse in Antigonish County. But Kim quieted him by saying that when Tim took Ghost to horse shows, he'd probably win every class — and everyone would know what a great deal her father had made.

Tim led Kim and Ghost down toward the river and turned right, up a path Kim had seen but had been too afraid of trespassing to explore. The trail, once a farm road, was now a deep green tunnel through mature spruce. They walked steadily, the thick springy moss underfoot muffling their steps. Saucy red squirrels chirped and skittered along branch avenues overhead. A ruffed grouse drummed a log nearby, a sound so deep Kim could feel it in her chest before she heard it.

The route took about twenty minutes. Neither of them spoke — there seemed no need. When they arrived at Hug a Horse, Vanessa accompanied them to the stall by the tack room. On the door was a handmade wooden sign in the shape of a horse. In elegant green letters it read

"The Ghost Horse of Meadow Green."

"Margaret made it for you," said Vanessa. "She said all pedigreed horses have to have long names."

Ghost circled his new stall, snuffing the walls and whinnying to the horses outside.

"He's a very fine horse, Kim," said Vanessa. "I'll introduce him to the others one at a time. In a few days he'll be out with the herd."

Then Kim and Tim and Jelly Bean made the hike back. Jelly Bean seemed to like her new home and calmly grazed without even looking around.

Tim told Janis he'd like to come back for the ceremony. Janis said he should just stay — have lunch, too. Tim wavered until Janis mentioned the fresh pan of brownies. "But I'm not dressed for a funeral," he said.

"It's not a funeral," said Janis. "It's a celebration — a homecoming. Casual dress is a must."

After lunch the adults drove to Erika's. Tim saddled Jelly Bean and led her down the road with Kim aboard so she and Jelly Bean could get the feel of each other again. Kim dismounted at the river pasture gate. A small crowd had gathered: Colm and Janis, Mr. Cameron and Lillian, Erika and two women in practical shoes and wide sun hats, both childhood friends of Lou's. Mr. Bell came, too. And Vanessa, Margaret, Lana and Michelle.

Janis asked everyone to stand in a circle. Colm started to read a eulogy for his mother, but he got too choked up to finish. Kim had sworn she wouldn't cry and make a fool of herself, but when the first tears she had seen Colm shed started rolling down his cheeks, she wept as well. Janis finished the reading and then gave everyone one of Gramma-Lou's memory stones. Next she sang Gramma-Lou's favorite song, "Small Victory" by Garnet Rogers. There wasn't a dry eye when the last note drifted over the river.

Kim mounted Jelly Bean. She took the blue urn with Gramma-Lou's ashes in her right hand and the reins in her left. Her heart pounded against the effort not to cry and her sudden fear. What if Jelly Bean started going too fast? What if she jumped the brook like Ghost had done and Kim tumbled off and Gramma-Lou's ashes got dropped in the manure pile? How would Gramma-Lou feel about that?

Kim knew the answer. Gramma-Lou would laugh. She'd laugh so hard she'd fall off the horse herself.

Kim nudged the pony into a trot. As she bounced along, she turned the urn on its side and slowly shook out its contents. A hand of wind gathered up Gramma-Lou's ashes and swirled them high in a soft gray sigh, out and over the sloping green field with the line of spruce trees and the river beyond.

Then Erika quietly took out a small black-and-white photo of Domino and put a lit match to one corner and let the ashes follow her friend's. She spoke softly, musically, of how Domino had lived in this pasture for twenty-three years. He had lots of children visit him during that time, but he always had a special fondness for the blond ones. He died of old age and was buried in the highest corner of the field under the maple trees he so loved to stand beneath. Over the years, people often said they still saw him standing there.

After the ceremony, everyone was invited to Kim's house. Margaret, Lana and Vanessa went home, but Michelle and Tim stayed on till suppertime, listening to Mr. Cameron and Lillian tell funny stories about Gramma-Lou and her days at the racing stables. Erika and Mr. Bell told their share of horse stories as well. The adults stayed through supper and late into the evening.

Kim went to bed to the sounds of lively conversation and foot-stomping laughter. She slept like a stone beneath slow waters, deep and still and silent.

On Monday morning, Kim went to school. It was grading day, the last day, and the first time in Kim's life that she didn't have to say good-bye to another school. When the bus door opened, it was also the first time she raised her eyes and saw the look on the bus driver's face. She knew that look. She'd seen it before — in the mirror, on Gramma-Lou, on Slug.

Fear.

The bus driver didn't hate kids. He was afraid of them.

Kim waved at Tim and sat two seats in front of the arrows. She had no wish to be anywhere near Slug. The Great Horse Trade story had spread, and Slug would know by now that Ghost was worth way more than the baseball.

The old bus rumbled into gear. Kim leaned her forehead against the window and stared at the horse that ran effortlessly alongside. Today he was golden — huge and golden with flaxen mane and tail. And Gramma-Lou was on that horse, her long golden hair streaming behind her.

And this time they ran for the pure joy of it, running toward, not from.